Also by Bryon Williams

Code Name 'Millicent'
The Cat Intelligence Agent who Came out of the
Cold

The Grumpy Old Withered of Oz

The Twilight Escort Agency

Tourist from the Light

The Burning Boy

The Reluctant Psychic

A Light at the End

The Psychic Spy

Not in the Public Interest

Naked Warriors

The Re-united

An Erotic Journey into Distant Realms

By

Bryon Williams

'A perfected man must have experienced every type of earthly relation and duty, every phase of desire, affection and passion, every form of temptation and every form of conflict. No one life can possibly furnish the material for more than a minute section of such experience.'

Source: Anon.

Chapter 1

For an artist of the senses, as Brendon liked to term himself, who appreciated form and light, space and line, warmth and sensual quality, which reflected in his work, his studio was perfect. Skylights and large, plate-glass patio windows opened onto a small balcony facing northwest, overlooking city skyscrapers, and in the distance the magnificent Sydney Harbour. The windows were fitted with an assortment of blinds, filters and fabrics and internal adjustable shutters for privacy and light control, which gave the impression of a space that could be minimised or maximised at will. Spotlights stood in a corner. Simple off-white walls with the slightest hint of flesh tones cleared his mind and stimulated his imagination and acted as a perfect background for the many evocative original paintings that adorned the walls. A row of black bookshelves containing the works of many brilliant philosophers and artist through the ages, stood against another wall.

Painstakingly restored pieces of aged furniture in a kaleidoscope of colours included a large, purple-silk-covered bed, breakfast and side tables, a couch, and several easy chairs which dotted the living room seemingly haphazardly. A pale green door opened onto a short hallway which halfway down led to a white tiled bathroom and walk-in robe, and at the end a functional if basic kitchen.

For the past year he had abandoned realistic land and sea scapes and was now going through what he termed his 'Still and Not so Still, Life Form' period. At twenty-five years of age, he had always been fascinated by the human form as an artist as was evidenced by the fine examples of erotica, framed and hanging on the walls, and unframed, standing in droves propped up against the bookshelves and walls like an army of sensual, naked warriors and their camp followers, too graceful and supine for battle.

As evidenced by several self-portraits concealed within the troop of provocative nakedness, his own self-portraits displayed the haunting yet strong, hard-to-ignore, masculine face framed with short, dark, unruly waved hair, which tended to form tiny curls at the nape of his powerful neck. Almost black eyes complemented by dark brown lashes and brows, confronting and yet always challenging and seductively inviting, almost stole the attention. The various positions seemed at times strictly posed and in other instances, vulnerable and almost withdrawn. His hard, naked musculature was a tribute to the long hours spent at the mixed sex gymnasium he frequented and, indeed, where he perused and eventually acquired many of the subjects as models for his current inclination towards his artwork.

One such model, Linda, whom he'd met and quickly evaluated at the gym while watching her lithe, supple body as she stretched and manipulated her glorious form on the horizontal bars, now lay naked on the dishevelled bed directly in front of the large window overlooking the city landscape with the sparkling blue ocean in the far background. He had adjusted a translucent curtain to throw a soft, glowing sunlight on her nakedness and scattered lavender, mauve and white hyacinth delicately on her perfect breasts and loins. But compelling passion had distracted him from his work at his easel and the blossoms now lay crushed and scattered as their bodies writhed and entwined in the enthusiasm of physical lust and craving: the perfume of their bodily exertions in their enthusiastic lovemaking mixing with the perfume of the blooms. Their breathing accelerated with their driving lust building ever closer to climax when suddenly he stopped, withdrew from her and quickly reached for a camera lying on a nearby coffee table.

'Come back, you bastard,' she groaned, stretching out her hand to him. 'Finish the job.'

He smiled provocatively and pointed the camera directly at her, snapping off quick consecutive shots capturing her demanding desperation and longing for satisfaction; her body abandoned and craving.

'First things first,' he murmured as the shutter snapped the images he would later use in the portrait he had already begun.

'I hope they don't turn up on Facebook or Twitter tomorrow,' she murmured sexily.

'No, but they may make the front page of the *Sydney Morning Herald*,' he replied, absorbed in his task. 'That should bring in a few bucks.'

'You're such a prick,' she laughed, 'but by God you're gorgeous.' Once again she took in the broad shoulders, the hard, rippling muscles of his arms and stomach, his still-erect penis and the overall beauty of his body as he stretched, ducked and weaved clicking away with his camera.

'Why, thank you, ma'am,' he joked as he focused. 'You're not all that ugly yourself.'

As he moved in for a close-up she came face to face with her nemesis, leaned forward slightly, reached out, and cupping her hand around his testicles, lightly ran her tongue over the head of his erection.

'Tastes better without the condom,' she smiled.

'Oh God,' he said glancing around the floor, 'it must've come off.'

She held it up with her other hand. 'I think we'll need a fresh one. I hate second-hand condoms.'

They laughed and he replaced the camera and took another condom from the bedside table drawer.

'It just so happens,' he said removing another sheath from the pack and waving it at her. 'Voila! Now, do you remember how this goes on?'

'I've practised on a few bananas but never the real thing,' she laughed as she took it from him.

'Well, you don't have to peel this one,' he replied, 'and if you wait a minute it will magically turn into a melon.'

'Ah, melon, my favourite fruit.' She pushed him playfully in the chest. 'But I do prefer it with whipped cream.'

'Cream coming up,' he laughed as he climbed back on top of her 'but you'll have to whip it yourself.'

Later, when Linda had returned for her evening shift as manager and receptionist of the San Gimignano Italian restaurant, Brendon was back at work on the painting with a photograph of their encounter, which he had quickly downloaded and printed as soon as she'd left, and thumb-tacked to his easel. He decided to highlight her face and left breast with a lighter shade of the purple coverlet she'd lain upon, or been laid upon, and touches of deep green shades of oil for the shadows.

He stepped back, screwing up his eyes, to get the perspective of his work and glanced at the photograph as he continued to detail the desperation and longing of her expression and the dishevelled angles of her body as she reached out to him. He was generally pleased with the feeling it engendered but much more work was needed before it could be considered for his exhibition in a few weeks time.

As he was attending to some fine detail work on her mouth to capture the hunger she exhibited in the photograph, his front doorbell rang twice. Frustrated, he checked his watch, threw the brush onto his palette and wiped his hands on an oil-and-paint-stained cloth as he made his way to the door. Looking through the peephole and recognising his visitor, he swore softly to himself before composing his expression to a more welcoming one and opened the door.

'Hey, hi, Donald,' he said brightly as the visitor entered and gave him a quick high five and a blokey squeeze on the shoulder and a smile in return.

They'd met at the gym a few weeks ago and remembered each other vaguely from their University days, which had rekindled their association. Being two years apart and involved in different courses, they'd never become friends as such but had bumped into each other from time to time and Donald was quite well known for his football prowess. There was an immediate comfortable rapport between them and they chatted amiably. Brendon had suggested they have dinner together sometime and then forgotten the day.

'Hi, Brendon,' Donald replied. 'I'm not too early, am I? I got away from training sooner than I expected and didn't know how long it would take to get here with the traffic or what the parking would be like.'

'No, not at all, mate, I just got a bit carried away with another painting I'm working on, that's all. Come on in, make yourself comfortable. Can I get you a beer or something?'

'That'd be great,' Donald said, walking past him and looking around the room before finally pausing in front of Brendon's easel. 'This is a really great place you've got for yourself.'

'Thanks, I like it,' Brendon said. 'A present I rewarded myself with from my Daddy's will. I think I deserved it considering I was the only child and he never had the time for me because thankfully he was more interested in making money. He was pretty well heeled.' And changing the subject, 'Hey, it was really a surprise catching up with you again at the gym. We didn't see all that much of each other at Uni.'

'Well, you were a couple of years ahead of me and we were in different courses,' Donald said, examining the erotic painting with a raised eyebrow. 'And what about your mother?'

'She died when I was very young and I was put into boarding school,' Brendon called out as he made his way to the kitchen. 'That's when my dad went into his own law practice and worked his way to the top. But I didn't really mind, we'd never been what you'd call *close*.' He gave a short, harsh laugh. 'Besides, boarding school was an education in itself. That's where I learned about life – well, my life anyway, and began to form my own opinions of this world. I studied philosophy and put myself through art classes, which gave me the basics, and then I spread my wings and flew. I got myself a sort of patron, a dirty old sod who was a friend of my father's, and eventually I was able to make a bit from the sale of my paintings for expenses so I'm doing all right.'

'Hey, is this one of yours?' Donald asked in obvious amazement, still studying the painting of Linda on the easel.

'Yeah,' Brendon replied dismissively, 'actually they're all mine', he said indicating the paintings hanging on the walls. I believe in self-promotion,' he said ruefully. 'I thought I'd mentioned at the gym that I had an exhibition coming up so I've been pretty flat out.'

'Yeah, you did mention you were an artist,' Donald replied, 'but I didn't realise you'd be quite this ...' he paused trying to find an appropriate word.

'Explicit?' Brendon laughed from the kitchen.

'Well, you did say you did life studies but,' Donald hesitated, 'I didn't think you meant, er, *real* life studies. I mean, hey, this is good – very good – very sexy.'

'Thanks. How was the training?' Brendon called.

Donald wandered idly around to a stack of canvases leaning against the wall and started to browse through them, his mind going into overdrive at the plethora of pornography he beheld at every flip of a canvas. He whistled softly in appreciation.

'Oh, pretty good,' he called back. 'The coach was coming down pretty hard on us and we were working our arses off for the big match on Saturday; semi-finals. Hey,' he continued almost without a breath, 'these are pretty amazing – very erotic. I don't know much about art but …'

'You know what you like, right?' Brendon finished for him with a laugh.

'Yep, and I'd say these are terrific,' Donald exclaimed. 'You're very into nudity, eh?'

'Yeah, somewhat,' Brendon replied entering from the kitchen and tossing a can to Donald who caught it expertly. 'The exhibition is called *Nudes of Night Dreams*.'

'Well,' Donald laughed, popping the can and taking a swig, 'your dreams are a lot more vivid than mine, I've gotta say.'

Brendon opened his beer and slowly sipped as he looked at Donald over the rim of the can. 'What, no wet dreams? You're obviously overworked on the footy field. I would've imagined with all that physical exercise and body contact you'd be hot to trot at a moment's notice. Maybe you're hitting the muscle-building steroids too hard. Too much can have a disastrous effect on your dick and balls, y'know.'

'Hey, no, not for me,' Donald said, shaking his head. 'I get my condition from eating the right foods, getting plenty of exercise and body building. And I've never had any complaints about the size of my dick, I'll have you know.'

'Well, your efforts do you justice,' Brendon said, sizing him up speculatively and shrugged. 'Maybe we'll make some comparisons later, eh?'

Donald actually blushed. 'Hell,' he smiled nervously, changing the subject and looking at his watch, 'are we going to eat or not? I'm starving.'

'Sure,' Brendon replied quickly finishing his beer, 'I've just got to take a quick shower and change. Make yourself at home.'

He stripped off his paint-stained and torn tee shirt and dropped his jeans leaving himself naked except for a pair of brief Calvin Klein underpants. Stooping to retrieve his discarded clothes and tossing them on the bed, he said, 'Go through the stack of paintings if you like and let me know your favourites. I like to get an outside opinion before I make my final selection.'

Donald watched the strip performance and laughed. 'Speaking of performance-enhancing drugs, you look like you'd have trouble passing the urine test.'

'Not me, man, clean in body, mind and spirit.' Standing and looking like a modern version of Michelangelo's *David*, he added, 'And I've got the test results to prove it.'

With that, Brendon disappeared into the bathroom. Donald continued sipping his beer as he made his way to the stack of canvases and began to examine them more closely. After a few minutes he strolled thoughtfully to the window, picking up Brendon's clothes off the bed as he passed. He stood admiring the view as the sun began to set behind the horizon.

Without undue thought, he absentmindedly lifted the sweat-stained clothes, looking for a laundry basket, and unintentionally inhaled the masculine odour. Suddenly he quickly turned and threw the clothes back on the bed.

Chapter 2

The restaurant was becoming crowded as Brendon and Donald entered and waited in line to be seated. Eventually Linda, looking very businesslike wearing a smart black tailored suit and white ruffled blouse, returned to the queue after having seated a middle-aged couple. She recognised Brendon and Donald standing a few places down the line and smiled, holding up her hand to them.

'Mr Barton, your booking is available now if you'd like to follow me.'

Brendon returned her smile and nodded as he ushered Donald past the somewhat impatient waiting customers in their wake.

'I didn't know you'd made a booking,' Donald whispered out of the corner of his mouth.

'I've a permanent standing booking with Linda,' Brendon smiled back with a wink.

Linda led them to a corner table beside the front window which looked out on the busy street and after they'd made themselves comfortable, handed them both a menu.

'Linda,' Brendon said gesturing to Donald, 'this is a friend of mine from Uni, Donald Leyton, and Donald, this is the lovely Linda. I've never had anything but satisfaction from her service,' he said winking at her.

Linda glanced at Brendon with a mischievous smile and shook hands with Donald automatically sizing him up.

'A pleasure, Donald. I think I may have caught sight of you at the gym. You're only new there, aren't you?'

Donald nodded and returned her warm smile, almost shyly. 'Yes, only a couple of weeks. I usually train at the club but I like to get away from all that muscle and butch jocularity occasionally.' He automatically checked her out and approved of what he saw. 'In future I must obviously pay more attention to the clientele. You do seem familiar, though, so I probably have caught sight of you there. I'm a bit of a freak when it comes to body building and exercise,' he continued self-deprecatingly, 'and tend to give it most of my attention.'

'So I see,' she replied, appreciatively.

Brendon smiled as Donald opened the menu and began to study the offerings. Linda was at it again.

'What's on the specials tonight?' Brendon asked, glancing up at her with a smile.

'Well,' she replied, 'this afternoon's special, the Chicken Breasts caressed with cream sauce, isn't available this evening, I'm afraid, as it seemed very popular and went down well – or so I was told. But I can recommend the veal scaloppini with mushroom and caper sauce.'

'Oh,' Brendon sounded disappointed, 'you know breasts are one of my favourites. So when can we expect them back on the menu?'

'I'd say you could look forward to that dish with a few improvements, say, next Wednesday?' she replied, invitingly

'Well, I'll definitely be looking forward to that taste thrill but I suppose until then I'll have to wrap my lips around a decent piece of meat,' he said as he folded the menu and handed it back to her with a smile.

Completely unaware of the innuendos flying over his head, Donald made his decision. 'I think I'll settle for the pasta with pesto sauce and a salad,' he said, handing back his menu.

'I'll send your waiter right over to take your wine order,' she said as she returned his smile.

'Oh, just send over a bottle of the usual Merlot,' Brendon said.

She nodded. 'Well, enjoy your meal, gents,' she said and turned to Brendon, 'And I'll see you for the special on Wednesday, I hope.'

'Wouldn't miss it for the world,' he replied with a grin displaying white teeth that would send an orthodontist into a fit of pride or a sense of depression for the lack of any future work to be done.

With a puzzled look, Donald watched her as she walked away. 'I think I do recognise that girl from somewhere,' he mused. 'It must be from the gym, it couldn't be from here. I've never been to this restaurant before.'

Brendon smiled. 'I doubt if you've seen her at another restaurant, she's been here for years. Started as a waitress and worked her ass off, literally, to get to manage the place. Maybe you've seen her picture somewhere.'

The penny dropped and Donald turned to him in amazement.

'That's not her, is it? I mean, the one in the painting? The one who was, you know …'

'Naked and in the state of coitus interruptus?' Brendon smiled, as he finished the sentence for him.

Donald blushed, which brought a flush to his cheeks and made his blue eyes seem even brighter. 'Yeah,' he mumbled keeping his voice low and quiet, 'the one – in your painting. But she sure looks a lot different now.' He turned to watch Linda efficiently greeting customers and escorting them to their table.

Brendon laughed. 'I would hope so. It could give the patrons a completely wrong idea of what the service entailed here.'

Donald relaxed and returned the laugh. 'Yeah, you can say that again. It would certainly take a few minds off their food. Well, you sly dog, my friend,' he said in admiration, 'you certainly have great taste in your women. She is beautiful.'

'I consider I have great taste all around,' Brendon replied. 'Beauty with a special inner quality always turns me on.'

'And what is her particular inner quality?' Donald asked, with a grin.

'Lust,' replied Brendon, 'pure unadulterated lust.'

Donald turned his head to watch the other patrons eating, chatting, laughing and obviously enjoying themselves, while Brendon studied him intently, slowly assessing him as an artistic subject as he did with almost everybody with whom he came in close or intimate contact. He saw much of the world he inhabited as a possible subject for his art, not only in form, line and shades of colours, but in the energy the subject emitted or projected. He could always sense an atmosphere or impression, a quality that exhilarated him or captured his imagination, and always attempted to portray that force in his work: sometimes in an impressionist style and sometimes in fine, realistic detail or a mixture of both.

Taking in the young, good-looking face and short, almost blonde hair that hung in wisps over his forehead, the large blue eyes still sparkling from his earlier embarrassment and the long, almost girlish eyelashes, his thoughts turned to composition. Great cheekbones and jaw line, strong, expressive manly mouth, he thought, and yet his countenance is nicely open and vulnerable, like a strong, virile young god who hasn't quite discovered the extent of his powers yet. There was no doubt Donald emitted a powerful, animal sexuality.

A sudden flash of memory and inspiration exploded in his mind. Yes, that's it: a young Greek god, like those magnificent figures I saw carved in marble at the Ancient Greek Sculpture Museum in Athens! The memory came alive in his mind's eye. He could just imagine Donald in another incarnation, marching off to battle or posing in naked glory for a sculptor after he'd appeared in the early Olympic Games; forever preserved for veneration. Brendon had been captivated by those glorious naked sculptures in their impossibly perfect beauty and detail of muscle definition in stone and the beautiful, proud or submissive women in peplos or chitons; soft robes draped in incredibly crafted marble folds that hung like soft chiffon from their smooth breasts to their beautiful carved feet and sandals. He'd spent hours wandering around the displays studying the figures marvelling at the sculptors' art and skill and returned day after day to be enthralled and enraptured.

Donald turned back to face him, catching the awed expression of memory on his face and was puzzled. 'What?' he asked.

Brendon's pictorial recollections immediately vanished but the image and longing lingered.

'How old are you, Donald?' he asked.

'Twenty-three,' Donald replied questioningly. 'Why?'

'Oh, I was just wondering,' Brendon replied vaguely as the waiters arrived with their wine and food. The wine waiter poured the dark red liquid into their glasses. Both waiters then withdrew.

They picked up their cutlery and began to eat. 'And do you have a steady partner – a wife or a girlfriend?' Brendon asked as he sipped the Merlot and slowly rolled it around in his mouth to clean his palate before attacking the scaloppini.

Donald's face became intent as he wound a fork full of pasta through the speckled green pesto sauce. 'No, not at the moment, I had a girlfriend a while back,' he admitted lightly. 'We met each other at Uni.'

Brendon studied Donald as he took his first mouthful of food and began to chew. 'And since then?'

'Oh, the odd tumble in the sheets – nothing serious,' Donald replied evasively.

'Nothing serious since the Uni romp?' Brendon sliced into the moist, pale scaloppini. 'I'm surprised.'

Donald looked a trifle distracted as he answered. 'No, our relationship was pretty much over. It wasn't working out. We'd both changed as we got older and it was time to move on. I wanted a career in football and she wanted to settle down and raise a family.' He swallowed. 'I wasn't ready. I wasn't really sure what I wanted.'

'That's perfectly normal at that age – that is, if anything is ever normal at any age.'

Donald looked at him quizzically. 'What do you mean?'

Not intending to sound too pontifical, Brendon quoted the theory of his personal philosophy. 'Well, I consider normality is purely the consensus of the majority forced on the many minorities to achieve their idea of what is acceptable and to give them protection, power and control over the masses,' Brendon rattled off. 'The various churches and many beliefs people are coerced and sometimes forced into are a prime example. But there are many and varied examples of subconscious manipulation of the masses wherever you look. Hype,' he said contemptuously, 'you see it every day in newspapers and magazines and certainly on television. It gives the majority a sense of respectability, a code they can live with; a living behavioural ritual if you like.' He paused, gauging Donald's stunned reaction. 'And there endeth the lesson.'

Donald was looking at him somewhat overawed, which Brendon took to mean he didn't understand.

'Normality is for the majority, the masses,' Brendon went on to explain more concisely, 'to keep them comfortable and secure in their moral behaviour and principles. But it does not necessarily apply to the free-thinking minorities who are bound to feel excluded, unacceptable or un-normal, if there's such a word.'

Donald laughed. 'Well, a philosopher *and* an artist, and also an anarchist, I'd say. You could be a dangerous man, my friend.'

Brendon grinned. 'No, danger and violence are not in my philosophy. But love, beauty and sex are as long as no one gets hurt intentionally. I just don't believe that all people should be judged by a single set of standards. Vive la différence.'

'So, let people do as they please as long as they don't do it in the streets and frighten the horses?' Donald laughed.

'Ah, you surprise me. You've been reading Mrs Patrick Campbell, or was it Bernard Shaw?' Brendon smiled.

'No, seriously,' Donald replied. 'Come on, you have to have certain standards to live by otherwise there'd be chaos.'

'And there isn't already? Read your history books, the papers, or worse still, watch the television commercials and news. The basics of kindness, respect, consideration, tolerance, and yes, unconditional love, are the only standards to live by. The rest falls into place.'

'Ah, and a preacher, too,' Donald responded. 'A man of many talents. You want to induct me into your subversive religion?'

'Good God, no,' Brendon scoffed. 'If I went into a church it would probably fall in on me.'

'So, are you trying to hit on me?' Donald asked sarcastically.

Brendon paused in his eating and looked at him squarely. 'And if I did, what would your reaction be?'

Donald blushed again, hating himself for doing so, and took another mouthful. 'I'd knock you back of course,' he blustered.

'Good. Well, that's that out of the way. You see, that is your choice. You have to be free to make your own choice in what is right for you without hurting anyone; what you personally will accept.'

'This is getting a bit heavy for a conversation over a meal between friends, isn't it?' Donald asked a little uncomfortably.

Brendon relaxed and leaned back in his chair. 'You're right. But speaking of hitting on you, I do have a proposition for you.'

'Oh?' Donald replied, curious but more relaxed from the change of tone the conversation had taken.

'So now we know where we stand, what's the proposition?'

Brendon picked up his fork and knife and once more attacked his food. 'Well, as you know and have seen, I'm an artist and at the moment I'm concentrating on the human form through civilisation for my next exhibition.'

'And?' Donald replied with a tinge of interest creeping into his voice.

'And I would very much like to paint you,' Brendon said bluntly.

Donald paused in surprise, another blush coming to his countenance.

'Naked?' he asked nervously. 'Like all the other painting you've done?'

Brendon nodded casually. 'Preferably'. He swallowed another mouthful. 'You'd be a perfect subject. You're good looking and at the height of your youth and beauty so to speak and that only lasts a few short years.' He laughed. 'And I think you have a body that would lend itself ideally to the image I have in mind.'

'And what exactly *do* you have in mind?' Donald asked, now with an edge of humour touched with suspicion in his voice.

'An ancient Greek god in today's world,' Brendon continued, unfazed by the insinuation. 'Perhaps wearing a football helmet, or maybe goalposts somewhere in the frame woven into an impressionistic background of an ancient Greek countryside, or Olympic racing track, maybe. I haven't decided yet. The ancient Greek athletes performed naked, you know. Women weren't allowed to attend.'

Donald fell silent, considering the proposition. 'Would I *have* to be naked?'

Brendon shrugged. 'You've seen my work and you've seen the theme so what do you think?'

Although surprised by the unexpected proposal, Donald's vanity couldn't help considering it. 'It's not that I have anything against stripping off. God, we're all buck naked in the dressing rooms and showers every week. But this would be different: one on one.' He thought for a moment, considering his options. 'Could I hide my face so I wouldn't be recognised? I mean if my footy mates were to see a painting of me in the raw I'd cop heaps of smart-arse remarks.'

'Are your mates likely to turn up at an art exhibition?' Brendon replied with a grin.

'Well, no, I suppose not,' Donald conceded. 'You'd be lucky to get some of them into the Louvre or the Prado.'

Brendon raised his eyebrows in surprise, 'You've been to Paris and Madrid?

'No,' Donald laughed, dismissively. 'I told you I'm from up north, from the bush. Never even been out of the state before I moved to Sydney. But Mum had a few art books lying around and I used to like going through them sometimes when I was a kid and look at pictures of the paintings. They were pretty incredible. That's why I was surprised when I saw yours. They gave me the same feeling.'

'Well, I'm flattered even if the compliment is a little over exaggerated. And what was the feeling they gave you?'

Donald shrugged, trying to recapture his reaction. 'I don't know … well, sort of *warm* inside. Some of them were tragic, sad, powerful.' He laughed in his embarrassment of revealing his inner feelings. 'I think I need another drink.' He reached for the wine bottle and refilled his and Brendon's glasses, pausing to give himself time to reconsider the offer. 'Still, you never know, maybe I'd go down in artistic history but … I don't know. I've never been asked to pose naked before to model for a painting,' he laughed.

'Believe me, you'll get the feel of it in no time,' Brendon assured him. 'You'll probably feel like you're relaxing in the club dressing room after a match. I'll even supply the beer. In fact, I'll probably have to force you to get dressed again.'

Donald smiled but still looked doubtful.

Brendon's face grew more thoughtful and exhilarated as the idea took hold. 'If you're going to feel uncomfortable about being recognised, maybe I could paint you so your face remained in shadow. Or, better still, maybe I could do the whole thing in mostly dark shadow, say a motley umber, with you in lighter highlights suggesting your muscles and face. Maybe that would add an extra mystery to the piece and the viewer could fill in the details in their mind: a sort of Rembrandt quality. In fact, I think you may have come up with an interesting approach.

'Now hold on a minute, mate,' said Donald holding up his hands. 'I still have to give it some thought.'

'Why don't you do that?' Brendon replied. 'No pressure, no demands, it's strictly your choice. But I will say I'd love the opportunity.'

Chapter 3

Brendon entered the studio followed by Donald who had obviously finished the bottle of wine to give him a bit of Dutch courage for the ordeal ahead.

'Come in, sit down, make yourself at home,' Brendon said with some excitement in his voice and manner as he hurried to a stack of blank and primed canvases in a corner of the room. He quickly sorted through them looking for the right size and primer colour. He discarded a black one and sorted through until he found a size that suited him, which was primed in dark gold.

'Ah, perfect,' he said as he held it up for assessment and satisfied, he attached it to an empty easel which stood nearby. He moved the painting of Linda to one side but still facing Donald who had flopped down into the sofa watching Brendon's seemingly frantic efforts. Brendon quickly stripped off his jacket and threw it on a nearby chair. He then quickly removed his shirt, leaving him bare-chested with a sheen of sweat highlighting his magnificent shoulders, pectorals and well developed abs.

Donald looked surprised. 'I thought I was the strip act for the night?'

'What?' Brendon, distracted at the unexpected interruption, then realised the reason for Donald's question. 'Oh, I often paint in the raw. It gives me more freedom.' As an afterthought he added, 'And it might help to give you a bit of company if we're both stripped. You won't feel so vulnerable.' He suddenly remembered 'Beer!' and hurried into the kitchen.

Donald sat looking a bit bemused at first and then, resigned, pulled a joint from his pocket and lit it, inhaling. He held the dope in his lungs for a few seconds and exhaled feeling the effects of the drug almost immediately and then laid the joint aside on a small decorative dish on the coffee table and began pulling his blue knitted shirt over his head.

In the kitchen, Brendon pulled open the refrigerator door and removed a couple of cans of beer, placing them on the kitchen bench to open them. As the second ring pull was removed he suddenly stopped, beer foam oozing from the hole in the top of the can. He reached up to the cupboard above, opened the door and removed a small packet. The label on the front read, 'Cialis'. He opened the packet and withdrew an orange foil sheet of little orange tablets and using his fingernail, he popped one of the pills from the foil and it lay in his hand. Carefully he dropped the pill into one of the beer cans and was about to replace the packet in the cupboard when he suddenly changed his mind and released another pill from the foil and dropped it into the other can.

'Hmm,' he murmured, 'that should release his inhibitions and compliance. Now all we need is Linda to drop by unexpectedly and this could be a very interesting night.'

He took the beers back into the studio, handed one to Donald and noticed the joint smouldering on the coffee table.

He smiled to himself, glanced at Donald who indicated that Brendon should help himself. Brendon accepted the invitation.

Amused that they would probably soon feel the effects of the marijuana on top of the Cialis, he quipped, 'Well, this'll put lead in your pencil.'

Donald grinned and took another swig of beer.

'Right.' Brendon suddenly unbuckled his slacks and let them drop to the floor. 'Off with the gear and then we'll sit back and relax and have a nice chat before we get down to business; two naked guys bonding.'

Donald chuckled and slipped off his loafers and socks, unzipped his slacks and dragged them over his hips where they joined Brendon's on the floor. He flopped back on the couch, mock-toasted Brendon and took a long swig of the ice cold beer and they shared the joint.

'Now, that's a lot better, right?' Brendon laughed.

'I'll be too high to pose standing up,' Donald chuckled.

'Maybe I'll have to change the title of the painting to "Pissed and Posed in Pompeii",' Brendon laughed.

Later, Brendon had laid out the palette and oils on his workbench as they continued to chat. He then moved to the light switch and lowered the dimmers, then adjusted the drapes and shutters creating an intimate, dim, eerie atmosphere. He hit the CD player button and the strains of Ravel's 'Bolero' wafted softly through the room. Moving back to his workbench he chose a series of tubes of oil colours including Brown Umber, Burnt Sienna, Brown Oxide and a warm yellow and squeezed a sample of each onto his paint-stained palette. From the selection of brushes standing in a large glass holder he selected a wide forty-five-millimetre brush and a smaller twenty-five millimetre one and laid them next to his palette. He quickly dipped the wider brush into a selection of the oil samples and lay in a mottled earth-coloured background on the canvas. Satisfied with the effect, he stood back and squinted his eyes and glanced up at Donald who was reclining on the couch watching him. Brendon smiled at him.

'Almost ready for you, my friend, don't go to sleep on me. I'll do a rough impression first and fill in the detail and highlights later. I work pretty fast at this stage so drop the jocks and let's get you into position.'

After a slight hesitation, Donald eased his briefs off, threw them on a nearby chair and stood naked in all his youthful glory. Without even looking at him, Brendon went to his desk drawer and removed his camera which he held up to Donald.

'Hope you don't mind, mate, but I have to take a couple of shots to work from while you're not here.' Donald went to object but Brendon hurried on to reassure him, 'Don't worry, they're not going to be made public, they're just for my work. They won't turn up on some gay website or Twitter or anywhere.' He laughed. 'I'm not into splashing my subjects on the public domain. If I got that reputation I'd never get another subject to pose for me; not my scene at all. I like to keep my subjects for my own personal reference. That way my paintings stay exclusively original. It's all part of the mystery. Okay?'

Donald hesitated dubiously, briefly wondering if he should trust this man with naked images of himself, and then reluctantly relented. He turned with his back to Brendon exposing his well-muscled back and firm buttocks.

'Perfect.' Brendon focused the camera and clicked off a few shots from different angles. 'Now, turn slightly around with your face down.'

Donald complied slowly as Brendon continued to click the shutter.

'Now further around and just lift your chin a little and relax. I don't want a male model pose as such. I'd like to keep it as relaxed and natural as I can. Think of scoring a try or facing the opposition who are out to kill you. – Good, brilliant,' he breathed as he continued to click and capture different angles.

Donald began to relax and quite enjoy the experience as he let his mind wander to various situations he had faced on the football field. Without realising it he had almost forgotten he was naked and being filmed but his groin hadn't forgotten and his penis began to fill and become engorged with blood. His erection grew as he was filled with a glorious feeling of male sexuality and freedom. He eventually turned to face Brendon with a smile of power; a picture of perfectly developed manhood.

Brendon slowly lowered the camera and stood looking at the vision before him and the memories of the marble Grecian gods slowly resolved and flooded into his vision, morphing into the strong, confident, figure before him. His gaze took in the perfectly unblemished, fine, sun-tanned, youthful skin, the beautiful line and form of the figure in the dim light, and he was completely transfixed. The two men stared silently at each other with the driving rhythm of 'Bolero' in the background, heightening the moment.

Brendon's eyes wandered down to the enormous erection and he smiled. 'I'm going to need more paint, I think.' He laid down the camera and turned away back to his easel.

As if mesmerised, Donald slowly strolled over to Brendon and stood behind him casually looping his arm over Brendon's shoulder while watching him working on the painting.

At first surprised, Donald's touch brought an immediate response that induced an avalanche of exhilaration into his being. An amazing energy seemed to permeate the room with the dim lighting and the driving rhythm of Bolero. Brendon turned towards Donald and the two men looked deep into each other's eyes discovering a surprising but incredible magnetism between them, which slowly gave rise to a realisation of a mutual inevitability. Slowly, Donald leaned forward and placed his lips gently on Brendon's. Brendon felt an overwhelming attraction and the strangest sensation of a long lost – what was the feeling? – familiarity?

He pulled back slightly, his heart beating faster and breathing heavily but unable to break the gaze.

'Are you sure this is what you want?' he whispered hoarsely, unable to shatter the mood.

Donald's reply came in the form of a deep, lingering kiss that began gently and gradually built into a powerful, hungry passion of entwined tongues and enduring kisses and caresses which slowly travelled down Brendon's taut body over his chest and nipples to his now urgently throbbing penis and testicles.

Chapter 4

In the morning, Brendon woke early, just before dawn as was his usual practice. Donald had obviously left but his scent remained. Brendon's mind immediately returned to the previous night and he attempted to examine his feelings. There was no doubt an exciting phenomenon had taken place; the strength of which he had never before experienced. This was not just a pleasant sexual encounter; this was much more. This was idolization almost worship. He was a deeply spiritual man who had developed his own philosophy on life which included individual expression coupled with regular morning meditation at dawn, facing the rising sun, which he felt connected him to his inner being, his soul.

But this morning his dreams and reality became confused with each other. He was certainly aware of the reality of last night lying with Donald. He remembered the kisses, caresses and passion he felt and what he somehow sensed, subconsciously, as a joyful reuniting of a relationship so long denied.

There had only been the amazing face to face physical and sensual pleasure of touch and taste without anal penetration, which neither had indulged in out of unspoken consideration for the other; neither wanting to dominate the other. It wasn't demanded by either party or necessary. Fellatio and touch had been sufficient to reach multiple unforgettable climactic orgasms for both partners through a long night. It was technically known as Frottage in the gay world.

This wasn't exactly the first such experience for him as he had often embraced intimate relations with both men and women without question, finding in each a different pleasure; neither taking precedence over the other. He had experimented with men as he believed the sex of the partner wasn't really all that important. He saw it as a sharing. He certainly hadn't been repulsed and in most cases found the experience quite pleasurable. It depended on the partner and what made them attractive to him and in return, him to them. With most male partners he thought no more of it than a mutual gratification, a shared sexual pleasure. He refused to accept the title of bi-sexual, a social term that offended him as did all labels, although it was probably technically true. He preferred to accept his tastes as a pleasurable physical and emotional gratification between two desiring people: each giving and taking pleasure of the other freely. But this was entirely different to anything else he had experienced. He certainly hadn't deliberately intended to seduce Donald. Or was it subconscious? He pushed the puzzling thought from his mind and reasoned that it was just a result of the mood he had unconsciously created with the lighting, the pulsing rhythm of the music and the intimacy of their mutual nudity.

He really should be up and meditating but his mind prevented him from rising. He lay back in the bed and thought of Donald and what his reaction might be to last night's encounter. There was a good chance he'd never see him again. He was probably furious with letting the situation get out of hand. Or would he be? Had he misread him? Mind you, the wine over dinner, the Cialis and beer and the shared joint might well have lowered Donald's inhibitions but maybe this was not an unusual encounter for Donald after all. Maybe if it was available he took what was offered. After all, Donald was a very beautiful and attractive human being; he must have numerous offers from both sexes. He had heard other men say jokingly of their sporting heroes, 'Gees, I'd turn for him'. But, from the body language and signs,

Donald didn't strike Brendon as a promiscuous closet gay or somebody who could have sex with another man willingly, without shame or regret, and Brendon suspected that the experience had probably shocked him out of his comfortable heterosexuality.

He had obviously tiptoed out of the studio well before dawn to avoid disturbing or having to face Brendon. Was that because of self-disgust or would he blame Brendon for what had transpired? If this wasn't a usual practice, Brendon suspected he would be very confused this morning and try to excuse himself of any responsibility, blaming Brendon for seducing him, which could certainly be construed as true, except it had been Donald who made the first physical approach. Brendon sincerely hoped Donald wouldn't blame either of them and see it for what it really was: two human beings sharing a special, beautiful, intimate moment.

But why did his mind insist on categorising the sensation as a 'rekindling' of a desire?

As for the painting, he had enough photographs to probably finish it and there was a definite driving force to complete the picture. But he secretly hoped Donald would return for at least another sitting.

Well, we should know soon enough, he'll probably never show up again, he thought, as he slipped out of bed and walked out onto the balcony to meditate. He sat in the lotus position facing the sunrise as was his usual practice and slowed his breathing. But the focus wouldn't come. Instead of calming his thoughts which, after years of practice, he could always manage quite easily, his mind's eye kept seeing Donald, naked and glorious, and the feeling of intimacy, and he could not dismiss the emotion that welled up inside him. Finally he accepted meditation just wasn't going to happen this morning so he went into the bathroom and showered and shaved. But the thoughts kept coming. *Would he ever see Donald again?* He knew there was something just out of reach he had to explore, but for the life of him, he could not think what.

His answer came sooner than he expected. He heard the front doorbell ring. Wrapping a bathrobe around his wet, naked body he padded to the front door and looked through the spy hole. Sure enough, it was Donald looking very contrite and subdued. Brendon opened the door to admit him.

Donald stood in the doorway with his hands behind his back, his expression inscrutable. There was an awkward pause.

'Hi mate,' Brendon said warmly, opening the door fully for Donald to enter. 'You want to come in or is that an iron bar you're holding behind your back?'

'No,' Donald said, entering and holding up a plastic shopping bag, 'Croissants. I thought we'd have breakfast together and talk a bit. But I'd prefer it if you got dressed first.'

'Right,' said Brendon, closing the door and heading for the bathroom and walk-in wardrobe, 'be right back. Why don't you put on the coffee and we'll eat before we talk, eh?'

Donald followed him through the door to the hallway and continued on to the kitchen as Brendon turned into the bathroom. Brendon heard the clatter of cups and plates as he quickly threw on a pair of pale grey slacks and a black sweater and slipped into a pair of comfortable black loafers.

By the time he re-appeared Donald had laid out the coffee and croissants on the small dining table in the studio. A jug of milk, sugar bowl, butter and a small dish of marmalade completed the meal.

'What, no muesli?' Brendon quipped lightly as he sat on one of the chairs that Donald had pulled over to the table.

'I'm not a fucking housemaid, you know,' Donald quipped back, wryly, and sat in the other chair opposite Brendon. 'Just as well in that fucking minute kitchen.'

'I eat out mostly,' Brendon replied, in defence, 'saves a lot of that housework stuff.'

He paused as he took a croissant, split it in half with his fingers and spread butter and jam on it. He waited for Donald to reveal his response to last night. 'You were up early,' he said, lightly, savouring the fresh croissant.

'I went for a long jog, well, a walk really,' Donald replied. 'I jog most mornings. But this morning I did a lot of sitting and thinking.'

'I thought you might,' Brendon replied lightly, as he licked stray marmalade from his fingers. 'And did you come up with any conclusion?'

They sipped their coffee in companionable silence for a while until Donald broached the subject that had obviously been playing on his mind and which had been the cause of his long session of introspection.

'First of all,' he said awkwardly, 'I want to apologise for what happened last night.'

Brendon smiled and shook his head. 'No need for any apology, we're both grown men and nobody got hurt. As a matter of fact, I enjoyed it enormously.'

Donald flushed and dropped his head to hide his embarrassment. 'Yeah, me too,' he said quietly. 'That's the problem.' He paused again and then almost blurted out, 'I want you to know that was the first time for me. I've always thought of myself as a normal heterosexual.'

'I hope I was gentle with you for your first time.' Brendon couldn't resist the temptation and laughed.

Donald's look didn't encourage any further smart-arse remarks.

'Really?' Brendon continued earnestly. 'I've got to admit that surprises me. I mean, look at you, you're not exactly ugly.' Donald flushed again. 'It's no big deal,' Brendon tried to assure him. 'I would imagine it happens more than people imagine in and out of the sporting profession.'

Donald shook his head. 'Not to me. I admit I've had the hard word put on me from time to time but I've always managed to avoid it; just evade it and don't talk about it.'

'Don't ask, don't tell,' Brendon quoted. 'That doesn't mean it isn't always lurking there. It's a part of human nature. It's just that most people don't want to accept it; too confronting. And, for the record *I* didn't actually put the hard word on *you.* '

Donald shrugged and tried to laugh. 'Latent homosexuality, eh? Bi-sexuality? Or mutual masturbation?' he said. 'A bit of M&M? Nothing like a mouthful of M&Ms, eh?' He suddenly grinned but his expression died and changed almost immediately to one of amused allegation. 'You had it planned all along, didn't you, since we met at the gym; the lighting, that bloody music …'

'"Bolero", by Ravel, a very beautiful and stirring piece of music. Torvill and Dean were responsible for bringing it back into prominence when …'

'I don't give a fuck what it was or who wrote it,' Donald broke in reasonably. 'You chose it because you knew the effect it would have and with the subdued lighting and the alcohol at dinner and afterwards when we came back here. I think it was a devious ploy to lower my resistance, get me in the mood, my free-thinking, sex-crazed friend.'

Brendon looked at him with the hint of a smile and shook his head.

'As a matter of fact, no. I always work in subdued lighting, and put music on when the occasion calls for it. Sometimes I work in bright light with rock music. I'm fairly catholic when it comes to atmosphere and sex,' he added.

Donald eyed him squarely. 'And nudity?' he asked.

'Mostly,' Brendon shrugged. 'I find it helps relax my subjects.'

'Ha,' Donald laughed. 'I don't think *relax* is the right word. Are you saying,' he continued, 'the whole night *wasn't* a set-up to get me into bed with you? The dinner, the lecture on being free to choose your moral behaviour, the wine and then home to get me naked?'

Brendon didn't mention the Cialis he'd slipped him to relax him and get his testosterone going. 'Free to make your own moral choice *as long as you don't hurt anyone,*' Brendon reminded him. 'Did I physically hurt you?' Donald shook his head and Brendon continued, 'I couldn't set out to seduce you if you weren't prepared or willing to be seduced. It happened and it was great, really great, and I enjoyed every minute of it. If it hadn't happened I would've got a lot more of the painting done though,' he smiled. 'Now I have to start from scratch again.'

There was a pause while he eyed Donald meaningfully, 'That is, if you decide to go on with it – your choice. And I might remind you it was you who actually made the first move. I just happily went along with it.'

Donald fell silent for a moment, his thoughts hidden. 'I take it this happens frequently?' he asked.

Brendon shrugged. 'Occasionally. Only when I find somebody I'm attracted to and they're a willing party.' He looked directly into Donald's eyes. 'You were willing, weren't you?'

Donald looked uncomfortable and avoided a direct answer. 'I admit, I woke up and felt, well, a bit embarrassed at first but then I looked at you sleeping and suddenly it felt … well, it was okay,' he said simply. 'That surprised me, I can tell you, and that's why I had to get out and walk and think. This will probably surprise you as well but I've never allowed myself to be put in that position before, I've never felt quite that way with a guy before. It was like I had no option.' Another long thoughtful pause. 'But I did,' he finished lamely.

'Actually no, it doesn't surprise me but in some way it proves my point.'

'What do you mean?' Donald said.

'Look, sex is an undeniable appetite and a perfect way to express attraction, affection or …' he paused, 'love with somebody. And yes I did,' he corrected himself quickly, '*do*, feel a great attraction to you. It wasn't just the wine or the music or lighting, there was more to it than that. There was something immediately that attracted me to you from the moment I recognised you again at the gym and I don't just mean your looks. Then, last night at dinner, I must admit I felt an uncomfortable desire for an *intimate bonding* to express my attraction to you but I would never have *put the hard word* on you or even broached the subject without your agreement.'

There was a moment when their eyes met and seemed to share a mutual acceptance.

'You must realise you are a very attractive person, my friend,' Brendon attempted to explain the unexplainable, 'regardless of what sex you are. You have an incredibly beautiful body and an amazing charisma and an animal energy that you project but apart from that there is a strange, mysterious quality about you as a person which for some reason I responded to.' He paused, trying to find the words to express himself without trying to sound fanciful and possibly destroy their growing honest relationship, 'It's like we'd met and been intimate before in some other time or incarnation. I desperately needed to capture that on canvas.'

Donald finished his breakfast, pushed back his chair forcefully and stood, looking a little stunned. 'You actually believe in reincarnation?' he asked as he walked over to the painting of Linda and stood staring at it.

'Yes, I do, as a matter of fact,' Brendon replied, as he wiped his mouth with a paper napkin. 'It's the only system that makes sense: the only belief that brings justice to the world. No man or woman can possibly meet all the challenges they face in one lifetime even if they manage to live out their entire physical life span. You make a decision and accept the consequences, either in this world or the next.'

Donald looked sceptical but Brendon continued. 'Yes, I believe that our soul reincarnates maybe hundreds of times into the situations it needs to explore and experience and in many cases to resolve or overcome a previous relationship. It's the only way our soul can develop and rise to a union with a greater divinity. I suppose you think that's pretty wacky but that's my form of belief.' He waited for the expected derisive reply.

Donald turned to face him with a look of stunned surprise, pausing to consider if and how he should respond. Brendon watched the interplay of expressions on Donald's face in fascination and waited, sensing a very personal revelation was about to be shared.

'When I was very young,' Donald said quietly, 'my mother took me to an exhibition in the gallery here in Sydney. It was an exhibition of ancient art relics, Roman or Greek, I think. We went into a particular room that displayed paintings and artefacts of battle. They seemed somehow familiar. In particular a small bronze shield, and I swear I recognised it! I knew how it would feel on my arm: the weight and the balance. I turned away from it, really confused, and then I noticed other weapons and paintings of battle. I was surrounded by them, and my mind started to spin and a darkness started to creep across my vision. I suddenly blacked out, fainted. My mother thought it was the heat or I was coming down with something and carried me outside to give me a drink of water. I never mentioned it to her or anybody else for that matter but the feeling of familiarity of those weapons stayed with me for quite some time. I did a lot of thinking about that incident after we returned home and for weeks later, and the familiarity of the objects I'd seen. Of course, I was a young kid and boys are attracted to weapons and war.' He thought about it for a few moments recalling the memory and then, receiving no reaction from Brendon, he continued, almost embarrassed.

'In my young imagination,' he continued with difficulty, 'I saw myself on a horse, as a soldier fighting fierce battles. I used to dress up in odd bits of rags and wield a sword and a spear and act out my dreams,' he laughed, 'but I suppose all boys do that and then as I got older, the memories faded and I put it down to my active imagination and gradually the dream faded. But I never forgot the feeling I experienced in that gallery. And then one day when I was in my teens I was in the local travelling library and I was sort of drawn to a book that was entitled simply *The Argument for Reincarnation*, and I couldn't put it down. It set me thinking.'

Donald blushed, which now seemed an uncontrollable habit, and mumbled almost shyly, 'I've never talked about this to anybody else before. I knew people would only laugh at me.' He raised his eyes to Brendon, 'Until now … with you.'

'*I think, therefore I am*,' Brendon quoted softly, 'An excellent argument for the existence of a soul. Descartes.'

'But as I grew older and saw the mess the world always seemed to be in I came to the conclusion that I've spent a lot of time thinking about the obvious inequalities in life,' Donald continued, 'living in the isolation of the country as an only child with very few friends and those I did have I could hardly discuss the subject with them. There seems to be such an order in life, in animals and nature – the Universe – that we take for granted so why isn't there some order in mankind? I'm not entirely convinced; I suppose because my mother was a very staunch Christian with very definite religious opinions. She probably brainwashed me while I was being raised. But despite the indoctrination, I've never actually shied away from the idea I just put it out of my mind. The question is just too big.'

Brendon went to his overflowing bookcase and ran his finger along the shelves in search of a particular volume. Having found it he extracted it and handed it to Donald.

'You might find this interesting,' he said.

Donald looked at the title and read the word, *Awakenings.* He looked up into Brendon's dark eyes. He suddenly felt as if he'd been handed a key to a mystery that had plagued him.

Brendon placed his hands on Donald's shoulders and looked resolutely into his eyes. 'You have a fine, enquiring mind, my friend,' he smiled. 'I sensed all along there was more behind that beautiful face and body than the mind of a country yokel whose only aim was just to run around tossing a football around a paddock, tackling and beating up the opposition, only thinking of proving your prowess as an athlete.'

'So you thought I was more than just a pretty face?' Donald facetiously returned the smile.

Brendon pulled him close and hugged him, '*Much more, my friend.*'

Donald pulled away, not entirely comfortable with the physical contact yet. 'Ah, let's keep this conversation purely on a non-physical basis, can we?'

Brendon smiled as he released him. 'Not an easy thing to do with you, I'm afraid.'

Despite himself, Donald felt a weird contentment with being attracted to this man, which, from habit, he would have automatically resisted, and quickly changed the subject. 'And what about Linda?' he asked, eyeing the provocative portrait, 'did you feel a previous relationship with her?'

'Well yes, of course,' Brendon replied, nonchalantly. 'Almost the same feeling I had with you. Except, a strange thing happened last night in that restaurant. While I was sizing you up as a possible model, my mind flew back to a museum I visited in Athens and the wonderful marble sculptures I'd seen there. They reminded me of you. That's what made me immediately think of you as a young Greek god.' He broke into a playful grin. 'Strange coincidence?'

Donald's face grew pale.

'But Linda and I definitely have a history we have to work out.' Brendon adroitly changed the subject as he suspected Donald was becoming too uncomfortable. 'I feel a very strong, almost uncontrollable lust for her but without the intimacy I felt with you. Maybe she and I have to equalise that lust from another incarnation: maybe that's the only thing that kept Linda and me together before, in other lives.'

'And what about your other "models"? Did you have a "history" to work out with them?' Donald asked as he idly browsed through the collection of portraits while attempting to resist the impulse to embrace Brendon.

Brendon shrugged. 'Some of them, probably. I only paint people I feel some connection with.'

Donald chose a painting of a naked, wrinkled old man and held it up to Brendon. 'And what about him?' he asked with a smile. 'Lust?'

Brendon laughed. 'No, but I learned an awful lot from that wonderful old man – Jeremy.'

'Such as? Donald asked.

'He taught me how fleeting youth is and how to take advantage of it; how the passion and vitality fades with time. He'd obviously been an attractive, arrogant young man and from his reminiscences, had screwed around a lot with anything in or out of a skirt. But he gradually came to the realisation as he aged that it just wasn't worth the effort anymore. The attraction that had driven him on for years could no longer give him a hard-on. At first he was bitter and found it hard to accept and hit the Viagra but as he aged further he came to realise it just wasn't as important as it had been and gave in to it. But he remained bitter that his youth was gone and his physical body was deteriorating along with his sexual drive. He was broke and needed the money. I paid him a fee for his next drink.'

'So that's why he looks so defeated, sad and morose,' Donald said studying the sagging muscles, the downturned mouth, heartbreaking eyes and other deep ageing lines so honestly captured in the painting. A wilted olive wreath sat askew on his head like the picture of an ancient fading Roman Emperor. 'I hope I go before that happens to me,' he said.

'I guess that's in all our minds,' Brendon said, 'but we have to accept that all matter deteriorates and only the soul escapes the ravages of time. Well, to a degree,' he added returning to his theory, 'depending what you do with the experiences. So, mate, I believe we have to make the best of our youth in the widest variety of experiences and leave old age for reflection and further contemplation and development of the soul. Forgive ourselves for the choices we made in the haste of youth and see them as a lesson to learn; experiences to absorb.'

'I'm all for that,' Donald said, thoughtfully, but then his face broke into lascivious smile. 'And what about this one?' he asked as he held up a beautiful nude portrait of a middle-aged woman tastefully draped in a transparent gauze veil over her face, in shades of blues and greys.

'Ah, that was Sylvia,' Brendon said, with an amused smile, 'my Widow in Mourning. A very wealthy socialite who also wasn't giving up her youth while there was a cosmetic surgeon on the planet. She had a very wealthy husband in real estate, luckily. She'd had more parts replaced than an old Mercedes. But she still managed to run smoothly and get her share of litres to the mile. It kept her husband in line because he was certainly running up the kilometres on the odometer; had the odd panel-beating job as well and a steady supply of Viagra to keep them both young. He died of a heart attack on the job. But have a look at her eyes.'

Donald looked more closely, not having particularly noticed them before.

'They're hard and proud, aren't they? Like she's saying, "I'm rich, successful, proud and still beautiful",' Donald said in amazement. 'I hadn't noticed because you've softened the expression with that veil and directed the eye to her posture and the overall effect.' He looked at Brendon. 'Did you have to screw her?'

'Of course, 'Brendon replied, as if the question was rhetorical. 'She needed to feel she was still attractive to young men physically, but she was a lousy fuck. Desperate and acting as if she were doing me a favour: always sure of the angle she presented even when we were screwing and makeup an inch thick – I hate makeup on women. I need to see the inside of the house not just the fabricated cladding. But she flatly refused to remove it so I softened it with the veil.'

'And these are definitely fuckable,' Donald said, holding up a picture of two beautiful, dark-haired young women.

'Ah, Roxy and Stephanie,' Brendon said with a lecherous smile, 'two nurses I met while I was in hospital with an infection.'

'What sort of infection?' Donald asked with sudden obvious alarm.

'No, not *that* kind,' Brendon laughed. 'A really bad flu. They were very amenable to having their portraits painted,' he continued. 'I thought they were going to be a pushover but they insisted on posing together and they didn't seem to be interested in a threesome unfortunately.'

'Lesbians?' asked Donald, with what could be only described as a smirk.

'No, I don't think so,' Brendon replied, candidly, as he continued his painting preparations. 'Well, there were no indications of it but of course you never can tell unless they're pretty obvious about it. Actually, they were two beautiful young ladies, in every sense of the word. They'd been friends since schooldays. I remember them both coming into my room at the hospital at the same time. They were very perky and bright and somehow strangely intriguing and I immediately sensed they'd be right for my Persian painting. We got talking and I told them about my exhibition coming up and showed them a few water colour sketches I'd done while I was lying in the hospital bed. They seemed pretty impressed and jokingly asked if they could model for me sometime. I didn't even have to ask.' He walked across and studied the painting.

'They were actually standing almost in the same position as they are in the painting, only fully clothed, of course,' he continued. 'My eyes stripped them, which, as you can see, they were probably pretty used to men doing, and then they shared that strange look of amused acceptance I think I managed to catch in the painting. So,' he paused, 'I asked them there and then if they'd be interested in posing naked for me, as a couple. That threw them. They exchanged a very interesting questioning look. They weren't shocked; it was as if they were asking each other if they dared and also for each other's approval. They then nodded to each other, without a word, and then to me. They agreed on the understanding it was for posing only with no sex involved and though it wasn't an easy promise to make, I agreed. We arranged a schedule that suited us all, they turned up together, and I finished the painting within a few days,' he said, simply. 'My brush just seemed to fly. I knew exactly how I wanted to paint them. It was all there, in my head.'

Donald looked at the picture in obvious admiration of the two dark-haired beauties standing almost opposite each other but slightly to one side, the front one half-obscuring the one behind, and turning their heads to face each other in semi-profile so that the girl in the foreground, Stephanie, had almost her entire bare back to the artist, with her long, beautiful, almost black hair tumbling down almost to her waist. Roxy stood behind her in an almost full-frontal nude pose, only slightly obscuring one magnificent breast with a very seductive dark pink nipple. The rest of their figures were perfectly proportioned and glorious in their nakedness and olive skin tone. But the outstanding feature of the painting was their legs: one leg of each slightly outstretched to one side and on each girl's leg was the most beautifully intricate pattern running down over their thigh from waist to the ankle. The complex design was so fine and delicate it looked as though it was etched in jet, gold and precious stones in a myriad of exquisitely transparent, jewel colours.

'Those tattoos on their legs are incredible,' Donald exclaimed in awe, 'and very sexy.'

'Thanks,' Brendon said lightly. 'They're not tatts, I painted them on later. They're based on an old Persian design I found somewhere. You'll notice the style of the flowers, leaves and the vine linking them are very unnatural but perfect in their artistry. The Persians certainly knew their art.'

'It looks like a very expensive piece of finely woven jewellery somehow glued to the outside of their legs.' Donald attempted to vocalise the beauty but found it impossible.

'They really went into bling in the Persian times,' Brendon mused, handing the painting back, distracted by his choosing the oil colours he was looking for.

Donald laughed as he replaced the painting and withdrew another picture, but this time, one of a sensual young man. 'I guess I don't have to ask if you fucked this one,' he asked with a knowing smile.

The picture was of a young, naked man, slim, dark, straight haired with a full, wide, smiling mouth. He was obviously of southern European appearance with dark glowering eyes. His head was slightly lifted in arrogance. He wasn't largely muscled but looked tall and well proportioned, with a limp but enviable eight-inch penis. His body was lithe and sensual with dark, curly body hair just beginning to appear and the shadow of a light stubble on his cheeks that gave him an image of manliness beyond his age. Brendon had used a variety of dark greens in the background and shadows to give the effect of outdoor coolness as if it were painted in the bush by a stream that expertly bubbled over the rocks. But strangely, in his hand he held a clay bowl which he was holding out as if tempting the viewer to drink. The portrait was quite mesmerising in its evil quality.

Brendon's expression hardened as he looked at the picture briefly and then dismissed it, moving back to his work table to continue rearranging his brushes and paints. 'I don't think I'm going to include that one in the exhibition. It doesn't fit the theme. The mood of the painting just came to me as I was painting it. That was Giorgio,' he said briefly, 'my example of modern youth and no, I didn't fuck him either.'

Sensing a mystery, Donald laid down the picture and asked why.

'I don't talk about all my models,' Brendon said glibly. 'Sometimes it's best to put them in the back of my mind and reflect on them at a later date: like when I'm old and grey, probably; like Jeremy. Now,' he continued brusquely, 'are we going to work or have you changed your mind?'

Donald studied him for a long moment, suddenly feeling more at ease in Brendon's company. He realised he really liked this attractive, and yes, strangely appealing young man with his weird ideas and he also admired the obvious talent he possessed. Surrendering, not unwillingly to what seemed the inevitable, he began to remove his clothes.

Brendon moved quickly around the room adjusting the drapes and lighting and directing Donald on where and how to stand. This time he selected another Ravel piece on his elaborate sound system and a beautiful piano concerto drifted through the dimly lit room.

'And afterwards?' Donald asked, with just a hint of provocation.

Brendon looked up at the naked Adonis before him and again felt a pang of repressed longing. He slipped off his own shirt. 'Jesus,' he said, as if resignedly, 'I've created a sex monster. We'll see if you need to get rid of any more inhibitions first,' he said as he picked up a thirty-millimetre brush and dipped it in the tanned, flesh-coloured oil. 'But now you know where I stand, I hope that's not going to be a problem.'

'You know, after our talk, I don't think it will be. I'm pretty cool with it now,' replied Donald. 'But all this standing still and posing will tighten me up. There's a good chance I'll at least need a good massage afterwards,' he smiled, wryly.

'Well, as long as you tighten up in the right area,' Brendon smiled as he began to apply the paint, 'that shouldn't be a problem.'

They soon became inseparable, playing golf, tennis, surfing and weekend camping: literally – and enjoying each other's company and interests as if they'd been intimate for years.

Chapter 5

Another painting Donald had asked about was a family study; a stout, middle aged father, James, an equally stout mother, Doreen, somewhere in her forties and their beautiful young daughter, Crystal, aged in her late teens or early twenties. All were stark naked and Brendon had arranged them in a stiff, Victorian period family pose with Doreen, wearing nothing but a beautiful example of Victorian millinery, decorated with a stuffed pheasant, which looked for all the world like it was sleeping peacefully amidst a Ming blue silk ruffle. She was seated on a carved, walnut Herter chair upholstered in grey patterned velvet, with James standing stiffly by her side wearing nothing but a black bowler hat. Crystal was an extraordinarily beautiful slim young woman with long, straight, blonde hair that caught the sunlight streaming through the window in golden hues and the clearest blue eyes Brendon had ever seen which gave the impression of a vulnerable, childlike innocence. Crystal wore nothing but a pale blue silk bow on the top of her head. At the parents' insistence, their daughter was half obscured standing behind her parents but her perfect young breasts and pink nipples peeked enticingly over her mother's shoulder.

The study was to be included in Brendon's exhibition depicting the development of mankind through the ages and one of his favourites. They'd had several sittings after Brendon had shown them examples of his work and explained his theme and ideas of producing it. At first reluctant, James and Doreen, who had been keen theatrical and hippy types in their youth, finally agreed to pose on the condition that Crystal was not over exposed in her naked entirety and would be demurely clothed in a robe during rest periods and toilet breaks. Brendon agreed but, on gaining their confidence and approval, had slowly managed to expose more and more of the beautiful Crystal, who didn't seem to mind at all. In fact, she managed to expose more than was originally agreed to, which delighted Brendon and often sent his penis into flights of unattainable fancy.

He soon discovered that Crystal was not unattainable and nowhere near the innocent virgin she portrayed in front of her parents as he subsequently discovered on several occasions, to his utter delight, when she slipped into his studio during the day without the knowledge of her parents and demonstrated the extent of her unanticipated, wild passionate streak. As usual he insisted she remove her artful but unnecessary makeup on arrival, which concealed the soft natural beauty underneath. At first she rejected his instructions complaining it would take too long to reapply but, at his insistence, she finally relented.

Her youthful naturally perfumed skin and long silken hair was sublime to his touch and caress and her lithesome body capable of the most exciting gyrations that too quickly brought him to an unusually uncontrollable ejaculation. When he groaned and complained about the swiftness of their coupling she replied, 'Well I only have an hour for lunch and I haven't eaten yet. And,' she complained, 'I have to reapply my bloody makeup.'

Unlike his experiences with Donald there was no love in their union but a virile and exciting lust and exploration but many times after Crystal had left, Brendon's thoughts inevitably returned to the extraordinary depth of feeling and perplexity he had developed for the handsome young footballer and wondered why and from whence it had derived. He had experienced a hitherto undiscovered passion enviable to a lot of men and women and yet deep in his being he still felt somehow bewildered, like there was a mystery over their relationship.

He continued his morning ritual of meditation but without success as Donald's image continued to invade his spiritual contemplation.

Although they had spent so much time together since their first sexual encounter, he had recently not seen or heard from Donald for several weeks; his calls remained unreturned or unanswered and he wondered if Donald had finally decided that their union was not acceptable to his choosing after all and had decided to end the relationship without notice. For the first time Brendon felt a strange emptiness in his stomach which even the previous enjoyable sexual exploits with the lustful Linda and the young Crystal and others could not dispel. Brendon had thought he had been in love before with members of both sexes but never quite like this. This was worship. Donald had captured more than his body or his heart, he had captured his soul and seemingly memories of a past long gone: a past that held desire, loss and sadness.

This is ridiculous, he remonstrated with himself, *why should this young man mean so much to me? It was almost like having one soul in two bodies.* He shrugged off the uncomfortable distraction and continued with the frantic work required for his exhibition which was now only a couple of weeks away and which would fall on his twenty-sixth birthday. He now no longer exercised what had become his sexual rite of passage with some of the models who sat for him and many were clearly disappointed. But he steadfastly threw himself into his work ignoring their sometimes overt advances and concentrating on the necessary task at hand which fortunately had only become a case of touching up, texturing, improving and framing.

He lined up the paintings in order of preference to relate the theme and impact on the viewer and was forced often to confront the painting of Donald which, by its spiritual strength and power, immediately took pride of place next to the painting of Stephanie and Roxy, but was yet unfinished to his satisfaction. There was an essence missing in his artful insight which continued to elude him.

The following Saturday he found himself outside the stadium where he'd noticed Donald's team was playing and, although not a fierce football supporter he felt compelled and impulsively bought a ticket and entered.

The atmosphere was intense and at the same time exciting and enticing with the expectation of the approaching contest. Brendon found his seat in the already almost packed stadium and studied the crowd around him: men, women and children of all ages joyful and laughing and vociferously discussing the prospects of each team. He observed the surrounding opposing team supporters wearing the colours of their idols, enthusiastically involved in the anticipation of the coming battle.

As he sat, the strident sound of the crowd enveloped him and his mind drifted into another realm, a realm of a forgotten past perhaps and he sensed the excitement of conflict and of battle to the death: near naked combatants sweating and straining for supremacy over their adversaries. Muscles glistening with sweat and blood, flashing swords and sicas, curved scimitars, and lances, round parma shields, or the oblong scutum shield: and faces contorted in victory, extreme, desperate effort or excruciating pain.

He was diverted from his reverie as the noise suddenly increased in velocity and the eighteen man opposing team ran out into the field led by their captain, Donald, who looked the epitome of a warrior leading his army into combat. The cheering minority of supporters almost being drowned out by the home team supporters who booed and catcalled as Donald's team ran into their prearranged positions, stretching and squatting to loosen their joints and muscles. The home team followed and the roar of approval from their supporters increased to fever pitch.

Brendon understood the rather simple rules of obtaining the maximum number of six point goals and the one point 'behinds' by, it seemed to him, almost any means short of punching, gouging or actually killing the opponent. The umpire moved to the centre square with, it seemed, the tallest two from each of the opposing teams with flanking ruckmen further out in support. The umpire bounced the oblong ball hard on the ground in what is termed, surprisingly, as a Ball Up. The ball flew high into the air and the centre four leapt high each competing to catch and kick or handball the football to his other team mates for advantage and the contest had begun.

The speed and agility of the players was mesmerising as they covered the field, leaping and crashing together to the roar of encouragement from the crowd and taking every opportunity to gain possession, running no more than fifteen metres before bouncing the ball or kicking or hand balling it to their team mates for heavily contested advantage. Donald, as captain was playing in centre position, directing the play with his two wingmen turning defence into attack and setting up offensive plays to help deliver the ball to the players in the forward positions where hopefully they could catch it on the full, thereby scoring a mark which would allow them the opportunity of kicking a goal through the centre two of the four white goalposts without physical obstruction from the opposition.

There were many disputes and appeals by both sides but the umpire's decision was never to be questioned and he controlled the play admirably, in some cases sending a player to the sin bin for a foul play which abused the sometimes confusing rules and brought forth a strong and vociferous reaction from the supporters. Brendon could hardly take his eyes off Donald who played intelligently and magnificently, guiding his team with skill and warlike determination.

By the beginning of the final twenty-minute quarter the score was slightly in favour of Donald's team and Brendon found himself caught up in the fervour and physicality of the game. He spent most of the time on his feet, urging on the efforts of his favoured player and roaring in approval at any hard-fought possession by his team. Unfortunately and unknowingly the seat he had purchased was in the middle of the opposing team's supporters and he received many angry looks and shouted, mostly good natured, insults as a result but he took them in good humour: well, his team was winning. At one stage Brendon would swear that Donald looked directly up at him and smiled but from that distance and with the throng of spectators, he considered it imagined and highly unlikely.

The result came down to the final minute of the fourth quarter of the game and the excitement was intense as Donald suddenly appeared astonishingly and seemingly miraculously to take a magnificent mark, despite strong interference from the opposing players, by twisting and levering himself like a mountain climber up an opponent's back and reaching high to capture the ball in mid flight. Even the opposition supporters roared their approval of this astounding feat. Taking his time, the concentration intense on his face, he stepped back a few paces and from fifty metres out from the goalposts and at an impossible angle, took two paces forward and kicked. The ball soared into the air and for a moment it looked as though it would surely float away to the left and miss the goalposts but in midair it swerved slightly to the right, correcting the trajectory and sailed high over the two centre goalposts for a match winning goal. The crowd erupted and the final siren blasted out signifying the end of the game. The visiting team had routed the home side and Donald was carried from the field by his team mates like the conquering hero he was.

Chapter 6

Brendon paused outside the exit door that opened into the corridor from the changing room watching the dispersing crowds and deciding if he should wait for Donald and then not wanting to look like he was stalking him, he turned and began walking back to the car park. Several players emerged before Donald appeared, still flushed from his success and no doubt, the cold showers. He was laughing and chatting with other team mates who were exiting with him. On seeing Brendon, Donald stopped and called out, 'Hey Bren, wait up!

Brendon stopped and turned to watch him laughing and signing autographs for the adoring fans whilst saying to his team mates,' I'll see you guys at the pub,' then he hurried to catch up with Brendon

'Hi, Bren,' he said affably, 'I saw you up there in the stands. You were really getting off on the game, weren't you?'

'Congratulations mate,' Brendon responded awkwardly as they shook hands, 'Terrific game, well done. Although,' he amended his statement, 'I reckon if all you guys played naked, you'd double your attendance.'

Donald laughed. 'You think so or are you a bit biased?'

'Probably,' replied Brendon, with a matching grin.

'I love winning.' Donald remarked.

'So I see,' Brendon replied. 'I thought you'd be good but I must admit, you were better than I expected.'

'Aw, shucks,' Donald responded with a mock expression of bashfulness, 'You want to join me and the boys for a few drinks?'

'Sure,' Brendon answered, surprised, 'but you deserve to share your success with your team mates and I wouldn't want to butt in.'

'Don't be an ass,' Donald replied, 'we haven't seen each other for a while and it would be good to catch up.'

They moved off in the direction of the car park chatting about the game and the close success Donald's team had achieved.

'Can you give me a lift home afterwards,' Donald asked, 'I got a lift in with one of the other guys.'

'Sure,' Brendon replied, surprised, 'No trouble, if that's what you want but I warn you,' he said, looking directly into Donald's eyes, 'my car might only get us as far as my place.'

'Low on petrol?' Donald asked innocently.

'No, but I think that's as far as I want to take you,' he said tentatively 'That is, if that's all right with you?' he asked hesitantly.

Donald paused, holding Brendon's gaze, steadfastly, 'Yeah,' he responded decisively, after a few seconds, 'I think we have some things to talk over anyway.'

'Oh, what sort of things?' Brendon asked, hesitantly

Donald paused again, wondering if now was the time to commit himself, 'Well for one thing, about how hard it's been staying away from you for the last few weeks,' Donald said quietly, as he stopped and glanced sideways at his companion uncomfortably. 'Look, I know this sounds completely crazy but I've come to realise I feel exactly the same way about you as I would usually, feel about a beautiful woman; only you're a guy!' he said, shaking his head in confusion. 'It doesn't make sense.'

Difficult as it was, Brendon resisted embracing him in such a public place but he knew exactly what he was talking about because he shared the same intensity of feeling. 'Well, with that we are in total agreement,' he answered with a huge relieved smile. 'I thought you'd changed your mind.'

'Don't think that's gonna happen,' Donald said. 'I've tried; I've been out with several women and even shagged a few of them but… it only left me thinking about you. This is just crazy,' he said, shaking his head in confusion.

He was prevented from elucidating any further as he suddenly pointed to where Brendon's blue Honda sports car was parked and pointed in alarm. 'Isn't that your car; the one those three blokes look like they're trying to break into?' Brendon quickly took in the scene of three hoons who looked like they were attempting to steal his beloved car with one attempting to hot wire the ignition and the other two acting as lookouts and yelled as he ran toward them with Donald in hot pursuit, 'Hey, you lot, what the fuck do you think you're up to?' Startled by their sudden discovery, the hoons' heads shot up in surprise and made to escape but Donald had foreshadowed their move and slipped around the back of the group, cutting off their escape, where he stood ready for action. Quickly realising their situation the hoons reacted, backing up together for safety, each assuming a defensive stance, their eyes warily appraising the danger they faced.

'Fuck off, poofs,' the heavily tattooed, apparent leader of the gang snarled, and raising the jemmy he had been using on the car, held it up, waving it threateningly. Suddenly, with a shout from their leader, the hoons made a run for it. But Donald and Brendon were too fast for them as Donald tackled one, throwing him roughly to the ground and belting his head on the bitumen surface and then, quickly recovering, regained his feet and threw himself at the other one who was attempting to attack Brendon from the rear. This hoon was no match for the ace football captain and was soon dragged to the ground. In the confusion of the attack, Brendon had hurled himself at the gang leader and blocked a blow from the jemmy being swung at him and punched the bastard heavily in the guts. The hoon gasped and bent over in pain at the heavy punch and Brendon ripped the jemmy from his hands and clouted him across the back of the head, knocking his assailant unconscious. Donald swung Brendon's other would be attacker around and kicked him viciously in the groin and followed up with knockout punches to his head, breaking his jaw and eye socket. The final aggressor's eyes opened in shock for a moment and dropped to the ground like a sack of potatoes joining the other two assailants.

Brendon and Donald, panting from the exertion, stood victorious, facing each other.

'Well,' said Donald, recovering his breath almost instantly, 'that should teach the bastards for trying it on with two pretty annoyed poofs,' he grinned. Brendon returned the smile as took out his mobile phone and dialled triple zero. 'Police please,' he said into the phone and when he was immediately connected, 'we've got a few would be car thieves here we need picked up. Oh, and you'd better send an ambulance. They're not looking too well.' He gave his name and location and hung up.

'I hope they arrive soon,' he said, 'I'm dying for that drink.'

They sat side by side at the bar sipping beer and occasionally chewing a handful of peanuts or potato crisps and discussing the short lived fight they'd just experienced with Donald's team mates. Sporadically their thighs would touch as Donald would turn to talk with his friends, and Brendon's heart would give a sudden jump at the pleasurable contact. Otherwise all appeared very normal and blokey and Donald introduced him to his team mates, referring to Brendon as an old friend with a wicked short stomach jab and who also just happened to be an incredible artist who had an exhibition coming up in a couple of weeks. The guys were fascinated to hear the details of the fight but it was clear that they were quite unimpressed with his 'hobby' as an artist.

'You see,' Donald smiled slyly, 'I knew they'd be wrapped with the fight but I can't see many attending the exhibition or buying any of your work. They might have a good ogle at your female nudes though,'

Brendon tended to agree with him and again wondered what it was that made Donald so different to them and with a sensitivity that only seemed to show when they were together. *Can we really know what goes on in other people's minds and what their tastes are,* he thought.

He often caught himself watching strangers and trying to deduce their lives and tastes and how they differed, how they lived and loved, what was their history? He also often wondered about their attitudes and what had shaped them. How much of their outward character was derived from their conditioning and how much they'd possibly brought with them from other lives. He was sure that everybody had had many previous lives and that they brought with them certain qualities they had developed through their previous existences.

When they arrived back at the studio, Donald walked in first leaving Brendon to close and lock the door.

'Well,' Donald said, almost before Brendon had joined him in the room, 'what's it to be: more painting or would you like to play around first,' he said, jokingly, beginning to unbutton his shirt. With the flood of adrenaline and testosterone still coursing through their veins from the football match and the fight in the car park, there was really little contest but there was still the condition that Brendon always stipulated.

'Your choice,' he said, his voice even but heavily influenced by his inner emotions.

Donald smiled in amusement and finally, managing to extricate himself from his sweaty shirt which was still clinging to his chest, he advanced on Brendon and began to undress him which encouraged Brendon to reach out and unbuckle Donald's belt, slip his slacks over his hips and run his hands longingly over his firm buttocks and muscled back in exquisite bliss. Naked, they embraced and once again the magic returned. Brendon stepped back to view Donald's body in all its masculine beauty and immediately noticed Donald's erection. His own penis had already started to respond as he continued to run his hands over Donald's body in a rising, uncontrollable, aching desire. There would obviously be no painting for a while yet.

Later, when their appetite and needs were depleted, Donald lay on Brendon's bed sleeping peacefully but Brendon was still awake reliving the incredible passion and completeness of their unbelievable union. He slowly rolled off the bed and stood looking down at his lover. Donald lay half on his back, completely uncovered, with one arm and one leg slightly bent and away from his body, his face half turned towards Brendon. The bed spread had been changed to a dark near earth colour and it now lay under Donald, ruffled and heavily creased from their torrid passion reminding Brendon of a rocky cliff from which Donald seemed to be emerging.

Suddenly inspiration struck and Brendon hurried to the easel and squeezed a large amount of complimentary colours onto his palette and took up his palette knife and began loading swathes of colour on the portrait's background. He manipulated the paint knife like a trowel, shaping and almost sculpturing it in the form of a rough stone cliff. He worked feverishly for some time reshaping and reworking other colours into the thick layer of paint recreating the effect he held vividly in his mind.

Suddenly he was distracted by Donald's languid voice as he woke and watched Brendon at work.

'Well, I suppose that's the answer, I've definitely turned into a faggot.'

Brendon looked up in irritation at the word that offended him and snapped, 'No labels and never use that word to describe yourself.'

'Well, if you must have a label I prefer pan-sexual, the attraction to both sexes. There are dozens of sexual orientations that you seldom hear about. More than fifty shades of grey in the rainbow. Do you know we could've been jailed for what we just did only as far back as 1997? We could've been locked up for twenty odd years with other sex starved men. Jesus, what an ugly, tattooed smorgasbord that would be.'

'They'd probably stick us in the laundry with the other deviates,' Brendon remarked, with a laugh. 'Social standards and conditioning change but the complexities in mankind remain, thankfully,' he retorted. 'Anyway I don't accept any label. Some things you can't put a label on and our relationship is one of them.'

Donald laughed. 'Let's call a spade a spade.'

Brendon laid down the palette knife and wiped his paint-covered hands.

'Do you know what percentage of men are gay in Australia?' he asked.

'No, I've never been interested enough to Google it,' replied Donald.'

'Well, even if you did you'd be fed confusing facts. For example, according to some statistics, less than three percent and in some cases, as low as one and a half percent of men in Australia openly classify themselves as solely homosexuals but I suspect there are at least another good percentage who are mentally still in the closet or *amenable* and won't admit it to themselves.'

'Well, I suppose that makes us members of a very small, elite minority,' Donald replied with a laugh. 'There goes our chance of marriage equality.'

'Is that a proposal?' Brendon asked with a hint of amusement. 'Anyway I don't believe marriage is a necessity; unconditional love and commitment and work through your problems, is my philosophy. Otherwise, if you're both up for it, go for it.'

'I wonder if that stat included the inmates of the men's prisons and the armed forces,' Donald wondered aloud.

'It's an almost impossible subject to get any real statistics on,' Brendon tried to explain and hopefully put an end to the conversation. 'For example, there have been many men who have shared and experimented with same sex relationships who don't and would never consider themselves as homosexuals and that's for good reason: not because they're in the closet and won't admit their occasional lapse but because they're still attracted to women. The majority of men in this age are repulsed by the idea and could never understand same sex attraction and frankly I can't see that changing in the near future.'

'I don't really care about other men's habits any more, only ours,' Donald said, rising and sitting on the bed, 'but it is very strange seeing I've never been inclined that way with another guy.'

'Sometimes it happens because of a lack of opportunity with their preferred opposite sex or maybe they find themselves in a situation where they're in mortal danger and rely on the extremely close and intimate relationship with their mates for their safety or even their lives. Without any real conscious thought, because of the nullifying danger or close reliance on each other they can find their testosterone levels rising rapidly and suddenly realise they're feeling incredibly horny and desperate for intimate contact and relief. In most cases, when they return to their *normal* previous lives, they revert to their preferred sexual partners of the opposite sex.'

'Do you think there's a chance that will happen to us?' Donald asked.

'Like I've said before, sex is a very strong appetite,' Brendon continued, 'and sometimes, under certain circumstances, some men get hungry and in desperate need of a satisfying meal so they dine out. You see that need every day when you look at some of the downright ugly couples obviously getting off with each other, like repulsive, mating blob fish because that's all they expect or that's on offer but it eventually loses its appeal and they revert to being discontented with the constant familiarity but let it drag on because of the brats they produce or because they have no other option apart from a messy divorce.'

Donald thought this over for a while but many questions remained unanswered. 'But we aren't in mortal danger and neither of us is actually a blob fish or short of available sexual partners of the opposite sex,' he said, thoughtfully.

Brendon looked at him squarely. 'It can also be the expression of a great and lasting love,' he said meaningfully.

Donald's expression seemed to agree but confusion still reigned supreme.

Brendon sighed and attempted to reassure his intimate 'partner of the same sex.' 'Has it occurred to you that you just might be discovering a bit of your more feminine side?' he asked. Donald shrugged unconvinced, 'Listen, are you or have you ever been aware of being attracted to other men?' Brendon asked. 'Do the guys in your football team for example ever turn you on say, when you tackle some guy and find yourself lying on top of him wrestling for the ball, group hugging when you've kicked a goal or when you're all undressing together, or in the showers? '

Donald considered this and found the answer coming up in the strong negative.

'Well, no, 'he said, 'not in the least. We're mostly only thinking about the game and the athletic contest. But on the other hand some of the pretty young groupies definitely turn me on. So how come I'm so attracted to you? I mean, just being close to you sends my head reeling and my hormones racing.

You've got to admit it's got to be considered pretty unnatural.'

'That's another term you should take out of your vocabulary,' Brendon replied, as he slathered more paint on the canvas. 'What is "natural"?

'Well, like most other people; men and women who are attracted to each other, sexually, I mean.'

'Did you know thousands of years ago it was considered quite natural for men to be lovers; sexual partners? The Romans, the Persians, Greeks; Spartans, as an example, are supposed to have even encouraged it, maybe even demanded it because when the soldiers went into battle they fought alongside each other and their emotional and sexual relationships encouraged them to protect each other and fight more determinedly. But they still took wives and had children.'

'Really?' Donald was amazed. 'So why did the practice become taboo and frowned upon?'

'It's always been there in a lot of people only most people feel uncomfortable talking about it,' Brendon said wryly. 'As we became more 'civilised' and 'socially conditioned' it fell out of favour I suppose and the church has a lot to answer for that. And the Victorians also have a lot to answer for. Middle class morality as George Bernard Shaw described it.'

'Have you been to church for confession lately?' Donald laughed, 'or were you ever an altar boy?'

'I rest my case,' Brendon said dryly. 'All I know is we all have a masculine and feminine side and sometimes, and under certain conditions, it can get,' he searched for the appropriate word, 'out of whack.'

'And that's your medical, technical term for it, is it?' Donald laughed.

'"Out of whack" – Google it, my friend, or look under Psychological Conditions of Homosexuality,' Brendon replied and continued with his painting.

Chapter 7

Clifford Angus, Brendon's agent, stood in the middle of the studio transfixed by the row of twenty-five paintings lined up in front of him. After a long scrutiny he took a deep breath and let it out. 'Whoo,' he exhaled in astonishment, these are *very* good! I knew you were moving away from the land and seascapes and still life and moving into your life form period, but I must say I never expected this… They're beautiful and very powerful.' He tore his eyes away from the line of paintings and turned to Brendon who was anxiously standing nearby waiting for his opinion. 'I think this is the very best you have done: certainly the most erotic.'

Brendon smiled in satisfaction. 'You think they'll sell?' he asked.

Clifford paused, his eyes returning to the paintings. 'Sell?' he exclaimed. 'Like hotcakes', he replied confidently. 'In fact, I can think of quite a few collectors who are really going to go ape over these.'

Brendon's smile widened into a grin.

'It will actually be a pity to split them up.' Clifford continued as he walked the length of the display. 'They deserve to remain in the order you've placed them. They create a wonderful continuous pictorial story of the development of civilisation with an almost hazy spiritual quality.' He returned to the beginning and stopped in front of the portrait of Donald which occupied the first position of the line-up and scrutinized it. 'But this is my favourite,' he said in obvious admiration. 'You know it reminds me of Michelangelo's unfinished sculptures of the slaves in the Firenze Academia: the way the figure seems to be emerging out of the marble. Only this one seems to be fighting his way out of a rock cliff; resolute in his struggle to escape the stone: the strong, expression, the powerful, perfect body, his arm reaching out to the viewer for help.' He paused in his assessment, 'This one alone will make thousands.'

Brendon's reply hung in the silence for a moment before he said softly, 'No, that one's not for sale.'

Clifford turned to him in amazement, 'What? You are kidding. It's the centrepiece, only it's at the beginning; the utmost epitome of the display.'

Brendon shrugged and turned away from Clifford's disbelieving gaze.

'It's not for sale,' Brendon repeated.

Clifford continued to stare at him for several moments with a mixture of disbelief and exasperation. Slowly his expression faded into sly understanding,

'Oh, I see,' he said, with a hint of lechery, 'like that, was it – is it?

Brendon ignored the question and poured himself a glass of red wine which he'd opened earlier to hopefully lubricate Clifford's artistic approval. He held up the bottle of Merlot inviting to refill Clifford's glass. Clifford nodded and held out his empty, etched, crystal glass and Brendon refilled it without meeting Clifford's eyes. Clifford secretly felt he understood Brendon's reluctance to sell this particular portrait but merely watched him silently and thoughtfully.

'Well, how about you do a copy?' he suggested, 'you've still got a couple of days to the exhibition.'

Brendon turned away back to his workbench and replaced the bottle, 'No, I don't think so. This will stay as an original and a one-off. Anyway I don't think I could recapture the same quality. It was created in a moment of discovery that has changed, and is still changing,' he added softly.

'That will be an artistic disaster,' Clifford announced in sartorial tones, 'but it will be in the collection on display?'

'Oh, yes,' Brendon agreed, 'but it will have sold or a not for sale sticker on it.'

Clifford shrugged hopelessly, imagining the considerable commission he would be missing out on.

'Well, you're the artist,' he remarked, disappointedly downing half of his glass's content in one gulp.

'Yes, I am, aren't I?' replied Brendon brooking no further discussion.

Later that afternoon Linda arrived at her usual pre-shift time at Brendon's front door and was surprised to find it locked. She rang the door bell but received no response so she knocked loudly thinking he had forgotten to unlock the door as was the usual arrangement. After a long wait the lock finally clicked and the door opened to reveal Brendon, dressed in white slacks and a black, V necked tee shirt which could not conceal the broad shoulders and well proportioned pecs she knew so well.

'I thought you must've gone out and forgotten our usual appointment.' She said a little reproachfully.

'Sorry Linda,' he replied, a little distracted and resolutely blocking her entrance 'I've been very busy arranging the exhibition and – time ran away with me.'

'Well,' she asked, expectantly, 'am I allowed in or do you want the perv next door to continue undressing me with his eyes? ' she said, indicating a middle aged male neighbour watching her in obvious speculation as he stood in his own doorway with his head poked around the corner.

'Oh, sorry,' Brendon said, as he stepped back allowing her to enter, 'of course, come in.'

'A bit distracted today, are we?' She asked as she passed him, covertly running her hand over his bum. 'By this stage you usually have your shower robe untied and my blouse and bra off,' she laughed. 'Feeling a little fragile as well too?'

He followed her into the studio where she was waiting for him with the light of sexual expectation in her eyes. He stopped and just stood looking at her, taking in the beautiful, sensual face and the longish dark hair falling down to her shoulders and curling in wisps over her forehead, the fine line of her body in a dark blue, slim fitting frock and legs clad in sheer black stockings with high heeled sling back, open toed shoes that matched her dress.

'Well,' she said, expectantly, 'am I going to be posing or shall we just skip that and I'll just undress, lie on my back and spread my legs?' she said with a seductive smile.

Brendon weighed up his options and came to an unexpected conclusion.

'You look very beautiful today,' he said, 'but…'

She laughed ruefully. 'I know, the make-up, it's got to come off, right? Oh, you're such a bore with this make-up thing,' she continued as she made for his bathroom with her handbag. 'I know it gets messy and I end up looking like an overworked whore but I thought that might turn you on for a change, well, not for a change,' she corrected herself, 'ever ready like a battery, that's you my darling and oh, by the way, speaking of batteries, I picked up a rather fun little sex toy this morning at that adult shop in er, what's its name street,' she prattled on from the bathroom, 'you know, the one near the cathedral. I bet they get a lot of trade there from the Bishops and *lay-priests*,' she laughed at her own joke. 'I know it'll give you a hoot. Battery operated, and the most amazing shape and multi coloured. Wait till you see it.'

There was a pause in her sexual ramblings as she concentrated on removing her make-up base and eye shadow. His lack of response puzzled her and she appeared from the bathroom, completely naked and holding a vibrator in the shape of a lizard with glowing multi shades of scales, and suddenly stopped dead.

The room was empty and the front door was wide open.

Chapter 8

Brendon sat in Sydney's beautiful and peaceful Hyde Park near the magnificent Archibald Fountain. He always loved this fountain designed by the famous Frenchman, Francoise-Léon Sicard, in the clean lines of the Art Deco style and built in 1932 to commemorate the association between Australia and the French in World War One, the Great War to end all wars, which of course, it hadn't.

He once again looked up at the centrepiece, the glorious statue of Apollo, who represents the Arts and light and beauty, holding out his right arm as a sign of protection of all nature while holding a Lyre in his left hand, spreading his benefits of giving life to all Nature. Behind him, at his feet high jets of water spouted into the air, signifying the rays of the sun which awaken nature and signal men to go to work.

His eyes roamed over the smooth sculptured figures of Apollo's chariot horses, with water gushing from their flared nostrils, the goddess, Diana, Theseus vanquishing the Minotaur and the wonderful tortoises spurting jets of sparkling water over the surrounding sculptures. But, although not probably intended, an overall feeling of sexuality pervaded the monument.

He pondered the fountain for a few moments, walked the grassy lawns and paths while examining the terrain, passersby and his inner thoughts.

What was happening to him? He had always enjoyed Linda's company and the sexual pleasure they shared together. But he realised that's all it was: sexual thrill and excitement: a natural appetite for a healthy young couple. But since his first encounter with Donald, those particular sexual thrills and pleasure, as wonderful as they were in the beginning, just weren't enough anymore to satisfy his inner being, his soul. His union with Donald gave him that plus that strange sense of familiarity but from where and whence it came eluded him.

A sudden thought of something Clifford had said this morning sprung into his mind and he rose from the bench he had been occupying and walked off in the direction of Macquarie Street and the National Library.

He entered the building and immediately headed for the Visual Arts section, a place he knew well from many previous excursions, and examined the shelves for his literary quarry. After a few moments of searching he came across two volumes that interested him and took them to a desk for appraisal. He read the volumes voraciously, mentally storing the information. The more he read the more outlandish the theory he was forming seemed. Michelangelo and the Renaissance period had always captured his imagination.

In the meantime, Donald was occupied with a much more physical task as he trained and sweated with the rest of his team mates on the practice field. But in the middle of a particularly hard run, he pulled up to a sudden stop and with a pounding heart, a vision of Brendon flooded his mind. For no apparent reason, he felt a sudden stab of pain in his chest.

His coach called out to him asking if he was all right as it was obvious something had happened to the young captain but Donald dismissed the question lying he had a sudden pain in his leg, probably a cramp or corked muscle and asked if he could be relieved of further training until the pain disappeared. The coach, ever protective of one of his star players, agreed and Donald limped off the field towards the change room and the medical staff who recommended he take the rest of the training session off.

He quickly showered and dressed and hurried as fast as he could to his Toyota Land Cruiser, and quickly took off in the direction of Brendon's studio.

Screeching to a stop outside, he threw open the driver's door and hurled himself to Brendon's front door and pounded on it with his fist. After an agonizing wait the door opened to reveal a startled Brendon.

'What the hell's the matter?' Brendon asked in concern as Donald pushed him back into the hallway and closed the door.

'Are you all right?' Donald asked.

'Yeah, I'm fine, why?' Brendon asked, bewildered.

Donald heaved a sigh of relief and staggered into the studio proper, throwing himself on the sofa.

'What's wrong?' Brendon asked in concern.

'Oh, it's nothing, just a bit buggered,' Donald replied. 'I was at training and it suddenly hit me. I got this sudden pain in the chest; probably a stitch. I'll be all right in a few minutes, but when it happened I had a sudden, I don't know, panic attack, I suppose. I suddenly felt you were in danger or maybe injured.'

Brendon laughed and went to sit next to him on the couch.

'Look at me, I'm fine,' he laughed. 'But thanks for your concern.'

He leant across and gave Donald a manly hug around the shoulders. 'But listen, I'm really glad you came over because I want to show you something I hadn't noticed before. He got to his feet and moved to the portrait of Donald which was now leaning against the easel. 'Look at this' he continued, 'I went out earlier and when I returned home I discovered this,' he said, referring to the painting.

Donald rose from the sofa and went to stand by Brendon to look at it.

After a minute, he gradually leaned closer to study the picture. 'That's brilliant, when did you do that?' he asked in amazement.

'That's the problem,' Brendon replied, equally amazed, 'I didn't.'

The background of the painting, the rough textured rock cliff face, had subtly been changed and on close inspection, revealed tortured, distorted faces and naked bodies also appearing to be trying to escape from the restrictions of the cliff.

'That is amazing!'Donald exclaimed. 'And you say you didn't do it?'

Brendon shook his head in equal astonishment, 'No, I don't think so, sometimes when a painting dries, subtleties appear that you never intended. It's one of the weird and wonderful things about painting. You never always quite know what you're going to get. But I think this is wonderful, better than before even though it wasn't planned.'

'But those figures are so astonishingly clear and the more you look at them, the more seem to appear. It's fantastic!' Donald remarked, astounded.

He looked at Brendon unable to believe what he was seeing. 'And you say this isn't exactly how you left it? There was no one else here that could have been responsible?'

Brendon shook his head and then suddenly remembered walking out and leaving Linda earlier. 'Wait a minute,' he suddenly exclaimed. 'Yes, Linda was here, she came over for an afternoon romp but,' he hesitated, unable to continue, 'no, it couldn't be her, Linda couldn't even paint a fence and she was probably furious at me for skipping out without telling her.' He raised both hands to his head trying to rationalise what had happened.

'Well, there's your answer,' Donald replied. 'Linda obviously can paint and you never had the inclination to ask her and she thought she'd make a few alterations to your work because you'd been such a bastard to her. She certainly deserves credit for what she's done.'

'No, I know from her reactions to my work she hasn't the slightest appeal or talent for painting,' Brendon insisted, 'only modelling, at which she's terrific if you're looking for an incredible body and rampant lust.'

'Well, there's one way to find out,' Donald proclaimed. 'Let's go and eat at her restaurant and ask her.'

Brendon hesitated. 'Ah, I don't think that's such a great idea after what I did to her today. She is *not* going to be happy.'

'Come on, don't be such a wimp,' Donald said, as he grabbed Brendon by the arm and lead him to the door. 'We'll drop by my place so I can change and don't worry,' he reassured him, 'you're bigger than she is and if she comes the heavy I'm always there to back you up with my Karate.'

They entered the restaurant well before the usual crowd had gathered and it was obviously a quiet night so far with only a couple of tables occupied by pensioners who liked to eat early and no queue waiting to be seated. Linda looked up from her booking list with her usual smile of greeting which died on her face immediately she recognised Brendon.

'Sorry, gentlemen, we're full,' she said, rather brusquely, and turned back to her reservation list.

Brendon smiled uneasily and glanced at Donald who appeared to be enjoying Brendon's discomfort.

'Look, I'm really sorry about this afternoon, Linda, but I had an urgent call – from my agent – about the exhibition,' he lied, 'and he wanted to see me immediately. I did call out to you that I had to go out but you probably didn't hear me.'

Linda looked at him speculatively and glanced at the now beaming Donald who was rather enjoying Brendon's awkward position. 'Funny, no I didn't hear you,' she said, obviously not believing Brendon's excuse.' She lowered her voice to almost a sarcastic hiss. 'Are you sure you didn't rush off to meet up with your handsome friend here? I know you like the odd departure from straight sex.'

Brendon looked uncomfortable and Donald tactfully stepped back and away from him leaving them space to work out their awkward situation. Brendon went to deny the obvious accusation but suddenly a door opened in his mind and he finally knew any attraction to Linda he'd had was now, at last, gone: that chapter of their history could finally close. He realised he'd only needed Linda as a model and they'd really only been using each other for sexual gratification with no real emotional attachment and it now seemed a shallow relationship which he no longer needed.

'Well, actually, no,' he replied, matching her quiet tone and realising it was time to set the subject straight. 'I didn't rush off the screw around with Donald, as a matter of fact but that really isn't any of your concern who I screw around with, is it? I think it's time we moved on from what we had. It was great while it lasted but I think we've run the course of any relationship we had, don't you?'

She responded with a shocked surprise.

'I know you well, Linda,' he continued, 'and if I'm not entirely wrong, you simply replaced the location for your regular servicing and moved on to one of your other conquests.' He looked around the restaurant and saw Richard, one of the waiters, tall, dark, solidly built and good looking in an obvious, continental stud style, who was watching them clandestinely while pretending to polish wine glasses. 'What I came to find out is if you messed around with my painting and ran off to Richard, over there, as my replacement? Or is his day a Tuesday?'

Linda was obviously surprised that he had guessed her liaisons with Richard but had fully intended making Brendon feel as uncomfortable as possible for as long as possible, believing quite wrongly it would give her more power over him in the future. However, apparently she had misjudged him and his reaction. She stared at him open mouthed. This was not the way she expected the situation to develop.

'Linda,' he said gently relenting, 'I know both of us too well. We were actually two of a kind. We took any opportunity we could to satisfy our urges and to be honest we were both pretty good at it. But that piece of karma is over and it's my time to move on.'

She stared at him, uncomprehendingly.

'We actually only came here to eat,' Brendon continued, 'and the restaurant is obviously not full, so do we get a table or not? We can go somewhere else if it's going to be too uncomfortable for you to feed us but before we go, I do have to ask you a question.'

Linda was shocked by his unemotional, calm and direct response and was at a loss for words.

'Did you touch my painting of Donald here, this afternoon? Were you lying to me when you said you didn't have the first idea of how to paint? Because if you changed it, it was obviously a lie. What you did to my painting was extraordinary for which I thank you but I object to anyone adding to my work without my permission, which I would never give, anyway.'

Still surprised at his revelations, she put the accusations of what she had considered were her secret infidelities to one side to deal with later and responded to his safer question. 'What the fuck are you talking about? I never touched that obviously gay-inspired piece of pornography. As soon as I realised you'd walked out on me *without a word*,' she emphasised, 'yes, I was rightly furious with you. Who wouldn't be? But touching your precious paintings never entered my head. If I'd thought of it I should've taken a knife to them and slashed them to pieces but I guess it didn't seem important enough.'

Brendon was puzzled and confused at her response and glanced at Donald, who smiled pleasantly at Linda. 'I'm available on Wednesday if you're stuck,' he said. 'Are you sure you can't find us a table?' he blatantly cajoled her. 'I'm starving and the food here is terrific.'

Linda was about to refuse but glanced over to the kitchen door to see the owner standing there watching with a quizzical look. She was forced to relent. 'Follow me,' she said curtly with a veneer of civility and picking up two menus, led them to a vacant table close to the entrance where she hoped they'd be disturbed by arriving customers and the blustery wind they would bring with them from the street. She almost flung the menus on the table and quickly retreated.

'Well,' Donald said, in amused satisfaction as he picked up a menu to eagerly study, 'that wasn't so difficult, was it?'

Ignoring his facetious remark Brendon glanced at Linda's retreating back.

'Donald, she didn't touch the painting and I'm pretty certain I didn't alter it. How the hell did it happen?'

'You said yourself,' Donald reminded him, 'sometimes the paintings take on a life of their own as the paint dries.'

Chapter 9

The exhibition was held at the famous Soho Gallery, in Cathedral Street, and the cream of collectors and art lovers turned up to see what Clifford described as one of the most exciting exhibitions he'd handled for many years. He knew his market and all the clients and critics that were worth knowing and who could afford to invest in a relatively new artist like Brendon.

With the help of the assistants and watched over by Clifford and the Director of the gallery, Nigel Messinger, the collection of Brendon's work was painstakingly arranged to lead the viewer, symbolically, from the beginning of civilisation through to the end. The first painting was the one of Donald which drew gasps from the crowd of admiring spectators. It was defined as a spiritual representation of reincarnation with the soul, or now souls, fighting their way out of a netherworld into an earthly existence, some willingly and some unwillingly. The crowds took some time silently admiring and evaluating the work before moving on to the next. There were also several whispered comments of disappointment but little surprise that the painting had already been sold.

They moved on to the second painting, 'Becoming', which was pure Expressionism or Fauvism mixed with a degree of Realism, in which he'd used a dark blue night sky background with the focus effect on translucent, elongated globes or globs as Brendon referred to them, seemingly hanging or dripping down the canvas and in each globe was the naked figure of a child, in various stages of development from embryo to birth. In each depiction the strongest feature was always the eyes, sometimes closed as in early development and slowly opening to the eventual birth to reveal the most innocent and vulnerable essence of the soul within.

It had a haunting quality which personified many of the works.

From there the viewer was led through the various stages of life from early babyhood to decaying old age and eventually, death, all of the subjects being naked with the occasional prop or piece of apparel depicting the various periods of civilisation through the ages. The earlier portrait of a naked baby was almost impressionist with only the hint of body shape and limbs but with the slightly overlarge, bright blue eyes of realism taken to its extreme. Mothers almost wept at the memories it engendered of the birth of their own children and fathers relived the unforgettable experience of seeing their child for the first time with an admirable inner self control. The final painting signifying death was almost a repeat of the style of the first one but in reverse with the globes seeming to follow an upward trajectory with each encompassing a human form disintegrating into a brilliant white light.

Donald entered the gallery alone and as soon as he approached the painting of himself, he pulled his sunglasses down over his eyes, turned up the collar of his jacket and pulled the beanie he was wearing down to his eyebrows trying to disguise himself in case he was recognised.

He heard a middle-aged, expensively dressed woman standing nearby whisper to her female friend, 'My God, I feel myself getting moist just looking at that gorgeous hunk of manhood,' to which her friend nodded and replied equally conspiratorially, 'Reminds me a bit of Stephan,' her head indicating her very plain husband nearby, a short, plump, balding man displaying an expression of complete boredom. The two women giggled and moved on.

When they reached the painting of 'Sylvia, the Mourning Wife', the naked middle-aged woman with the rich husband, the second woman exclaimed, 'Holy shit, that's Sylvia Simmonds! Well! The artist was certainly kind to her,' she continued bitchily. 'You can't even notice the plastic surgery scars and he obviously painted her through a gauze screen.'

'Or PVC plastic,' her friend retorted, giggling.

'I see it's been sold though,' replied the other woman. 'I'll bet Sylvia insisted her husband buy it. She wouldn't look that good in a photograph unless it was Photo-Shopped.'

'He did catch those money grabbing, manipulative eyes though,' the friend giggled.

It didn't appear that any of the other models, apart from Sylvia, had made an appearance which wasn't surprising under the naked circumstances. Linda was a no show but Brendon didn't really expect her to attend even though she and all of the models had been invited. The finished portrait of her in obvious sexual frenzy, placed further up from Donald towards the more contemporary scale, was extremely confronting and wouldn't resemble the chaste, businesslike image she went to so much trouble to project in public.

Donald quickly moved on and noticed Brendon at the back of the room, escaping the crowd of gaping admirers and heading out the door. He followed.

Clifford was busy circulating, chatting and bargaining, pouring white wine into eagerly outstretched empty glasses, trying to lubricate prospective buyers and admirers with a glowing expression whilst trying hard not to look too ecstatic at the prospect of the sizeable commission he was bound to receive.

Donald eventually caught up with Brendon, looking exhausted, lounging back in a chair outside the coffee shop nearby, sipping a latte.

'Hi, mate,' he said sitting opposite him and signalling the waiter for one of the same. 'Well it certainly looks like you've got a success on your hands in there – congratulations.'

Brendon thanked him but it was obvious he was a little overwhelmed by the reaction his exhibition was getting. 'It's a lot better than I expected I must admit or even hoped for,' he replied.

'Well, from the reaction I was witnessing, this is really going to put you on the map,' Donald said, removing his beanie and sunglasses.

'Oh, that's who you are,' Brendon laughed, pretending to recognise Donald. 'I didn't realise that was you in that funky disguise.'

'Thought I'd dress for the part,' Donald replied with a broad smile. 'And you can't talk,' he continued, 'look at you in your cool white jacket, open down to the third button with the gold chain and pendant around your neck and that bright red scarf *casually* tossed over the shoulder – *very arty*.'

'Showbiz, my friend, everything is showbiz nowadays.'

'And I thought tight fitting pale grey slacks were out,' Donald remarked, his eyes taking in Brendon's full outfit, 'and baggy, low slung pants showing the Calvin Klein logo on the band of your jocks and the crack in your bum was in.'

'Have you noticed the average age of the women buyers in there? Mid forties and older, the ones who fondly remember tight pants hugging a good rounded arse and a nicely filled crotch. Show-it-all-biz, baby.'

'You really have a Narcissus complex, haven't you?' Donald laughed.

They were interrupted by Clifford hurrying toward them and flopping into a chair. 'A long, strong, black,' he said to the waiter who was delivering

Donald's coffee and then turning to Brendon, beaming.

'Well, it's almost a sell-out in there, my friend, and I'd say it will be a complete success in another day or two with the number of holds waiting to be finalised. Are you sure you won't change your mind about the painting of this football bum,' he said referring to Donald. 'I've had literally dozens of offers to buy it from the "anonymous" owner. And we are talking, big, big money here.'

Brendon looked across at Donald and smiled, 'No, that one is definitely not for sale. That's staying in my private collection.'

Clifford looked enormously disappointed but was in no position to argue seeing Brendon had unquestionably made up his mind. 'Well,' he shrugged disappointedly, 'it's your decision, of course, but it's a shame. You will let me know if you change your mind, won't you?'

'Yes, of course, 'Brendon nodded, 'but don't hang by your balls waiting.'

'Anyway, even with the current sales,' Clifford's spirits rose, 'this is going to make a very tidy sum for both of us.'

'How tidy?' Brendon asked.

'Many, many thousands,' Clifford replied, joyfully.

'Enough for a trip overseas?' Brendon asked, idly.

'I'd say, around the world a few times, first class, five star,' replied Clifford confidently. 'Why, have you got plans?'

Brendon looked at Donald thoughtfully. 'I think a trip overseas would be just the ticket at the moment,' he replied, non-committally. 'Frankly I'm a bit exhausted after the last few months and there are a couple of things I would like to check up on.'

'For another exhibition?' Clifford asked hopefully.

Brendon shrugged, 'Maybe, you never know.'

'Well,' Clifford said excitedly, 'that could legitimately be a tax deduction, you know.'

'Better and better,' Brendon replied, laughing.

'Where are you thinking of going?' Donald asked, a little disappointed at the thought of being separated.

'Oh, Italy, – Rome, Florence, Pisa, you know the usual tourist spots,' he answered hazily 'maybe further afield. I haven't decided exactly. Just want to get away for a while and rediscover myself.'

'Well, I think that would be an excellent idea.' Clifford announced. 'Europe is a great place for inspiration. I'll give you the name of some friends and acquaintances who can show you around if you like. I've got some terrific contacts in the art business over there.'

'Thanks Clifford, I'll let you know if and what I decide as soon as the money is in the bank.'

'Right,' said Clifford, standing and gulping down the last of his coffee. 'Now, I'd better be getting back to fleecing your admirers while they're still hot to trot, I suppose. You coming back in soon? There are still a lot of influential people wanting to meet you and I've had a couple of requests for interviews from the press and a couple of Television Arts' commentators so don't be too long.'

'I'll be in shortly,' Brendon assured him.

There was a long pause between the two remaining friends as they each contemplated the future. The awkward silence was finally broken by Donald as he stood.

'Well, I have to be going as well,' he said to Brendon. 'I'm due for a training session. We've got the finals coming up and we really need to up the stakes in training so I guess I'll be pretty busy for a while. I'll pick you up a ticket for the finals if you're interested? '

'Hey, that'd be great,' Brendon beamed, knowing how difficult it was to actually get a ticket for the final.

Donald tapped the side of his nose, 'Ya gotta have influence, my friend, someone on the inside.'

Brendon smiled indulgently, 'Will I be seeing you tonight? I'd really like to celebrate.'

Donald stood looking at his friend for quite some time wondering if this special relationship would soon be coming to an end now that the exhibition was over and with Brendon's plans for an overseas trip.

'Wouldn't miss it for the world,' he said, nodding as he held out his hand.

Brendon held the hand slightly longer than necessary and smiled warmly.

'Good,' he said, 'see you after training.'

Donald nodded again and stuffing his beanie and sunglasses in his pocket, turned and walked off.

Brendon's speculative gaze followed Donald's retreating back as he walked down the footpath admiring the effortless manly gait and secretly planning the future.

Chapter 10

The celebration was small; just the two of them. Brendon had chosen a very upmarket restaurant instead of the usual San Gimignano not wanting the distraction of Linda's disapproval again. They had both dressed appropriately in two piece suits, shirts and ties, each of a matching colour; Donald wore a blue shirt and matching tie and Brendon had favoured green. They looked like two expensively and fashionably dressed businessmen out for a meal on their expense accounts. The restaurant had a French decor and ambience with soft lighting and surrounding muted conversation. A grand piano played French music in the background

'Well, what do you think?' Brendon asked Donald.

'Very classy,' Donald admitted, looking around, admiring the surroundings and their fellow diners. 'Do they serve a pie floater?'

'Probably,' laughed Brendon, 'but it's sure to be under another name, say, *Un Flan Avec le Boeuf avec le Consommé des Legumes.*'

'Sounds *magnifique,*' Donald responded.

'Order whatever you want,' Brendon invited him, 'it's your modelling fee.'

'Oh, so it's not for sexual services rendered? Thank God for that. I'd feel like a hooker.'

'A very expensive hooker by the look of the prices,' Brendon said, running his eye down the price list.

'And you're saying it wasn't worth it?' Donald asked, with a sly smile as he studied the menu.

'Worth every franc,' Brendon replied, kissing his finger tips and throwing it to the sky, in the French manner. '*N'est pas*?'

Their pre-dinner drinks arrived and Donald raised his glass in salute, 'Happy Birthday, my friend, and congratulations on the success of the exhibition.' Brendon raised his glass in acceptance and smiled, 'Well, hitting twenty-six hasn't been so bad,' he said. 'I suppose it's downhill from here on in. Old Jeremy reminded me that we spend more years old than we do young, not a very reassuring thought.'

Donald laughed. 'Not you, mate, from what I've seen, and remember, you'll still be going strong in fifty years' time.'

'And then I'll probably be off on the big adventure again,' he replied, 'off into the cosmos and into a different realm of existence; a different dimension.' He paused thoughtfully. 'It's a pretty exciting thought, isn't it? I often wonder what other lives I've lived and what I've learned and what bought me to this place in this time. What's been our previous connection I wonder? I know in my very being this is not the first time we've been together. I felt it the moment we first met. It hit me like a thunder bolt. Whatever it was, I sense it was big.'

Donald laughed. 'Well, thanks for the compliment but I'm really only a little over the average length – not that I've actually done a lot of comparing,' he added quickly. 'This reincarnation business has really got you in, hasn't it?' he asked, in genuine interest.

Brendon nodded. 'Once I discovered it, it really intrigued me. I mean my curiosity really exploded. The whole purpose of life became clearer. I could see the justice in the way people acted and reacted according to the Karma they'd created and their soul development. I understood how we all really are part of the one existence, albeit it an unfathomable encompassing 'All', from the nucleus of an atom up and the thousands of existences we had to go through to get to where we are: and how we're all on an upward trend, not only materially but spiritually.'

'Tell that to the poor and starving of the world,' Donald replied sarcastically.'

'But don't you see,' Brendon replied earnestly, 'that's also part of the development we have to go through; to know what suffering is like, to learn compassion and love for each other, both the receiving and giving; to experience every facet of life to be able to grow, spiritually. No one existence can give you all of that experience.'

Donald mulled over the theory and though he was swayed by Brendon's argument, he was still caught up in the here and now. 'Okay,' he smiled, 'let's just take it one step at a time and see what develops: like eating and living now. Isn't that what we're supposed to be doing?'

Brendon laughed. 'Sorry,' he apologised, 'I do tend to get caught up in my philosophy. Yeah, let's eat, drink and be merry – and have great sex,' he added.

After the delicious meal and an excellent bottle of Charles Heidsieck Brut Reserve champagne and a lot of light, comradely repartee, the two men's culinary appetites were sated and sat back, replete.

'Well,' Donald broached the subject that had been on his mind since the exhibition, 'so you're off overseas?'

'No,' Brendon replied as he took a swig of his wine, '*we* are off overseas.'

Donald almost choked on his wine but managed to control the urge and swallowed. *'We?'* he asked in surprise.

'Well, I hope so,' Brendon replied. 'What do you reckon?'

Donald was flabbergasted and for the moment couldn't answer.

'Well, you don't expect me to go on my own, do you?' Brendon asked. 'What fun is that?'

'But I can't just go tripping around the world like that,' Donald answered in astonishment, 'and even if I could I've got the finals coming up next week and I couldn't let the guys down, could I?'

'I don't mean tomorrow,' Brendon replied dismissively. 'I mean after you've won the finals, dickhead.'

'But even so, I don't know if I have that sort of money to splash around,' Donald protested.

'Ah, but I do, or rather I will have, after I collect my share of the takings from the exhibition. That is, after Clifford takes his majority of the take.'

'There's no way I'm going to let you pay my way,' Donald said defiantly. 'Then I would *really* feel like a whore.' He shook his head in fierce denial.

'No, I couldn't let you do that. Besides, you won't make a brass razoo from the painting you did of me, you wouldn't even put it up for sale.'

'It wasn't because I was ashamed of it,' Brendon explained. 'I just wanted to keep it for myself. It means a lot to me,' he said, almost shyly.

Donald looked at him in disbelief. 'You're pissed,' he said, jokingly.

'No I'm not,' Brendon responded, soberly. 'I need you to come with me.'

'For God's sake, why?' Donald asked in amazement.

Brendon paused, gathering his thoughts and his argument.

'Did you read that book I gave you on Reincarnation?' he asked.

Donald sighed at Brendon's obvious obsession. 'Yes, as a matter of fact, I read it and… okay, I was impressed, but not entirely convinced,' he added, doubtfully, 'but… impressed.'

'Well, I'm *definitely* convinced and I think,' Brendon paused again, 'no, I *need* to know if we had any relationship or Karma in the past that would explain this incredible and downright unusual attraction we have for each other. I'd like to know if it was because of some other incarnation we shared and I have an idea where to look,' he said, 'but I need you with me.'

'But I can't remember what happened to me last week,' Donald exclaimed, 'let alone when I was a baby, and certainly not before that, and I bet you don't either, so how do you expect to remember someone you knew in another lifetime?'

Brendon looked at him askance. 'Did you read *all* the book? Didn't you understand that it's not our brain that remembers but our *soul*? You do believe we have a soul, don't you?'

'Well, yes, I suppose I do,' Donald replied defensively, 'but…'

'Look,' Brendon asked, decisively, 'have you ever been somewhere for the first time and had the feeling that you were somehow familiar with it? A feeling you'd been there before even though you hadn't? Or met someone for the first time that you immediately warmed to or avoided because of an odd feeling that you'd met them before and didn't immediately like them or even warm to them or something made you suspicious of them on a first meeting?

'Well, of course, everybody has that experience,' Donald replied, dismissively. 'I suppose that happened the first time I saw you.'

'Yes, me too, but some people are more sensitive than others, depending on their journey: their soul development, if you like. Well, I believe I may be a bit more sensitive, aware or more open minded than some people: I'm an artist, for Christ's sake, we're supposed to be more sensitive.'

'And a little whacky,' Donald added, with a grin.

'Maybe a lot whacky,' Brendon accepted. 'So, indulge me. Come overseas with me: I have a few places I want to visit and see if, together, we both feel any connection with certain places and if we do it could give us a lead. I need to know,' he said defiantly. 'But if it doesn't work out it will still be a great trip.'

'It can't be open-ended,' Donald stipulated. 'I do have another life you know, and I have to get back for pre-season training. I don't keep this magnificent physique without a shitload of work, you know,' he said jokingly.

'Jesus, I don't want you to get fat and sloppy either,' Brendon laughed, 'although I don't know if that would make any difference to how I feel. How about just for a few weeks? Surely you're allowed a bit of a break now the season's over?'

Donald studied his companion closely and couldn't help being moved by the conviction in his voice. He sighed in resignation, 'All right, if it's that important to you, I'll join you on your *spiritual mission* mixed with a lot of sight seeing if that'll make you happy but I've got to admit, I'm very doubtful about any great *spiritual epiphany*. I just think our relationship happened simply because we discovered we are both bi-sexual – sorry about the label,' he added quickly, 'and mutually attracted to each other.'

'Ah, but why?' Brendon insisted. 'That's the point I'm getting at.'

Donald shrugged helplessly and finally succumbed to Brendon's determination.

'Okay, where would we start on this *spiritual voyage of self discovery*?' he asked.

'I prefer to call it a journey into a distant realm,' Brendon replied, half pissed. 'It could be the chance to discover *us* and maybe what we were to each other,' he said earnestly, and then continued, 'I think first to Rome and then onto Florence and we'll see where that leads us.'

'You think we might have an Italian connection?' Donald asked incredulously. Brendon shrugged.

Despite his doubts, Donald couldn't help but be impressed and exhilarated at the prospect of visiting Italy for his first trip overseas. 'Rome? Florence?' he repeated in wonder. 'I've never been there or anywhere out of Australia.'

'Haven't you?' Brendon asked suspiciously, raising one dark eyebrow questioningly. 'Maybe you have and your brain's forgotten. Who knows what we might discover about ourselves.' He smiled happily, caught up in the mystery and anticipation of the forthcoming adventure and looked at Donald suggestively.

'Now, to more pressing matters, you want to spend the night at the studio?' he asked.

'Try and stop me, buster,' Donald replied with a grin.

Chapter 11

The finals match was even more exciting than the previous match Brendon had attended. The crowd was even bigger and, if possible, even more passionate in their response. The fans were nearly all dressed in their team's colours with some in funny, bright-coloured curly wigs and wearing striped slashes of coloured war paint and striped scarves and carrying placards or oversized red hands with upraised index fingers and hooters. It was ear-splittingly noisy with the cries of support or derision as the battle ebbed and flowed.

Brendon found himself sitting next to a much older, friendly guy and caught up in the near hysteria shouting support and encouragement with the best of them as the players ran and jumped and bumped and tackled, the game moving endlessly except for the short pauses when a player took a mark or for a ball up or when a ball was kicked out of play or an injury interrupted play. And of course the short breaks between quarters when the players would leave the field and the fans rushed for drinks or snacks to revive their flagging strength, which gave Brendon at least a short time to recuperate his energy and ponder the excitement he was witnessing.

Strangely, although both sides were made up of mostly attractive, muscular young men, many the image of perfect manhood, Brendon did not find any of them more than vaguely sexually attractive and even then in a detached way, except for Donald who featured heavily in a lot of the action. It was as if Donald was in the midst of a battle and he was determined to win and showed no mercy in attempting to achieve his victory.

This aggressive tendency surprised Brendon who had many times enjoyed his sensitivity and tenderness without once noticing the more belligerent side of his nature. It was as if it was only when they were alone together their moods complimented each other and they were confident enough to relax into their true natures without the need of the social masks people often adopted.

The game continued and the crowd once again rose to the occasion and returned with frenzied support of the players. The umpire's decisions were often loudly refuted to no avail, which didn't seem to upset the hordes unduly and in many cases brought derisive or genuine laughter. It was a spectacle

Brendon had never before encountered to this degree. But at the same time the charged atmosphere evoked strange, familiar memories which quickly evaporated into the recesses of his mind.

The athletic demonstration powered on at an incredible pace and as it drew close to end of the fourth quarter, the excitement grew in tension to an unbelievable climax. The score was once again slightly in the opposition's favour by eleven points but Donald's team were resolute and with another goal by Donald, the teams slowly drew closer to almost even the score to the delight of the supporters, who this time surrounded him, thanks to the seat Donald had organised for him.

Again a roar of encouragement erupted as the ball flew high in the air and the speed and agility of Donald's reaction was nothing short of amazing. With a dive through the air like a superhero in flight, Donald reached impossibly high and caught the ball for a mark and the crowd went wild. This time he took careful aim and kicked the ball directly to another team mate who was running across the field at great speed and in line with the goal posts with an opposing player close on his heels. The ball fell short of its mark and bounced awkwardly but the lead player anticipated the trajectory it would take perfectly and caught the ball. Turning his back to the nearby goal posts, he kicked it high backwards over his shoulder in a remarkable feat and sent the missile soaring over the centre posts to a one-point victory.

The crowd erupted in triumph and went wild. Brendon had gone hoarse from yelling encouragement and the victory roar. The old guy sitting next to him, whom Brendon had learned from their friendly exchange of conversation during the match was an ex-player himself, thumped his back in exhilaration and joy, hugged him and managed a kiss on Brendon's cheek. Brendon responded with a throat-scratching laugh and hugged him back and the two men instantly became friends. The losing team mostly sank to the ground in disappointed exhaustion and Donald's team ran or walked to the outer field in triumph to greet friends, family and ecstatic supporters with outstretched arms.

Then came the presentation of the trophies and many of the crowd, especially the losing team supporters, took the opportunity to escape the stadium and beat the throng to their cars in the car park. But Brendon stood and watched proudly as Donald, the victorious captain, gracefully accepted the trophy on behalf of his team. The love and admiration welled up inside him as he applauded loudly.

At the end of the ceremony, after the presentation of the trophy and the official photographs, he slowly made his way through the jostling, crowd toward the exit and on toward the change rooms at Donald's earlier invitation. The room was a riot of cheers and compliments as the winning players embraced, drank beer and champagne from bottles and cans and shook each other's hands, congratulating each other profusely and slapping each other on the back. Brendon stood in the doorway watching the well deserved celebrations. Suddenly Donald saw him over the shoulder of a team mate who was hugging him ecstatically and extracted himself with great difficulty. He walked to Brendon and they embraced in the usual manly fashion.

'Great job, mate,' Brendon congratulated him warmly and patted him on the back. 'That last manoeuvre was brilliant.'

'Right time, right place,' Donald answered, modestly, 'but it fucking worked, didn't it?'

'Like a fucking dream,' Brendon agreed.

'Come and meet the boys,' Donald invited him. 'They're all a bit buggered but feeling no pain,' he laughed.

They spent another half an hour with Brendon congratulating and chatting with the rest of the team and the atmosphere gradually returned from pandemonium to almost normal with guys getting undressed and heading for the showers and shyacking around, returning naked to dress back into their strangely out-of-place suits and ties.

Brendon idly watched them realising he was almost totally unaware of their nakedness and felt hardly any sexual attraction towards them at all even though he was aware of their male beauty in an abstract sense.

Finally Donald sidled up to him and said quietly, 'I'm off to the showers and then I'll get dressed and we can leave.' He leaned a little closer and whispered, 'Ya wanna watch?'

Brendon laughed and said, 'I think I can wait – just.'

'Good,' Donald replied, 'But I warn you, when we get home I'm gonna expect the best head job since Nureyev's farewell to the Royal Corps de Ballet.'

'You are definitely due for that, my friend,' Brendon replied, with a smile and immediately felt the stirring of a roaring erection.

Chapter 12

They arrived at the Leonardo Da Vinci, or Fiumicino International airport as it was commonly called and shuffled along with the line of other passengers through Immigration and Customs. Donald was quietly overwhelmed by the whole new experience of International travel and took the delay as a chance to look around, taking in the foreign surroundings and the multitude of different nationalities with great interest, although weary from the long, crowded flight and even though Brendon had splashed out and upgraded to Business Class seats, the time delay was still exhausting. Brendon took the hindrance of officialdom in his stride from previous experience.

They eventually collected their luggage after the usual delay at the carousel and made their way to the Leonardo express which would take them to Rome's Termini central train station. From there it was only a short walk to the Hotel Sonya directly opposite the Opera Theatre, which Brendon had booked on the internet.

They approached the front reception desk and Brendon gave his name to the desk clerk.

'Ah, yes,' said the clerk, 'a double room with queen-sized bed?' he said, looking up in query at the two men.

'Yes, that's right,' replied Brendon in a tone that brooked no discussion.

The clerk nodded without a flicker of censure and reached for the electronic key swipe behind the polished wooden desk.

`Room 332, third floor, *signor*,' he said, somewhat enviously, his smiling eyes quickly assessing the two attractive new arrivals as he handed over the key, 'and we hope you will have a pleasant stay, gentlemen. Please feel free to ask me if you need any assistance – anything at all,' he added with obvious undertones.

Brendon and Donald thanked him and headed for the elevator.

'Hey, nice place,' Donald remarked, '"anything at all"? Did I detect a hidden proposition there?

'Probably,' Brendon replied. 'Lots of *amore* in Roma. Just don't take advantage of it without a condom.'

They found the room and Brendon swiped the card key in the lock and opened the door into an acceptable, medium sized room decorated in a pale gold colour with a white tiled en suite. The room was spotlessly clean with a queen-sized bed with a dark brown patterned spread being the main feature. A desk stood in front of an adequate sized window that overlooked the street below with brown horizontal striped drapes and a wardrobe. A bench and large makeup mirror above, stood against another wall.

'Yes, this will be entirely acceptable,' Brendon said surveying the room.

'Acceptable?' Donald said laughingly. 'It's bloody luxurious in my books.'

They unpacked their bags and hung their clothes as Brendon explained their itinerary. 'First, we'll take a couple of days getting acclimatised and over this bloody jetlag and just relaxing and then we'll be off on the grand tour I've planned for us. It's wonderful just walking around Rome and we'll be doing a lot of that I warn you. Everywhere you look is an experience and the food and wine are brilliant.'

'Just the walk from the Termini was an experience in itself for me.' Donald said elatedly.

'You still got your wallet and passport?' Brendon asked jokingly.

Donald patted his buttoned cargo pants pockets in reassurance. 'Yep, I kept everything locked up tight as you kept ordering me,' he said. 'God, I kept my eye on anyone who came within ten metres of me. Who says I'm paranoid?'

Brendon indicated the small wall safe set above the bench. 'We'll lock our passports, travel papers, cash and spare credit cards in the safe they provided and keep one credit card each in our shoe ' Brendon laughed, 'and remember to keep your eye out for the gangs of street urchins. They're very good, very professional; they'll have your briefs off you without even taking off your pants.'

'I know, I know,' Donald groaned, 'I just cuff 'em and shout out *Via Via*! Which means fuck off, right?'

'Not literally, 'Brendon replied 'but close enough.'

That afternoon they lunched at a little local roadside *trattoria* and Donald was amazed at the way the cars were parked, sometimes wedged onto the sidewalk or so close together he wondered how they could possible drive off without ripping off a fender or at least leaving a dent or scratch on the bodywork.

'My God, they drive like maniacs,' he observed, amused, as he watched the constant stream of traffic passing through the crossroads.

'That's why we'll be walking and not hiring a car, 'Brendon informed him. 'You see more walking anyway.'

'That suits me just fine,' Donald said, tucking into the antipasto. 'I'd rather walk anyway.'

'And don't, for God's sake, order a cappuccino after breakfast time or they'll think you're a fucking tourist and overcharge you.'

'Where are we going this afternoon?' Donald asked eagerly.

'I told you,' Brendon sighed wearily, 'we'll just have a wander around and you can get the feel of the place first. The tour starts tomorrow.'

'Where to first?' Donald insisted.

'Well,' Brendon surrendered, 'I reckon the first place you've got to see is the Forum and afterwards we'll head across to the Coliseum, it's not that far away but wear your runners.'

'I'm a footballer,' Donald remonstrated, 'I sleep in my fucking runners.'

'Not that I've noticed,' Brendon smiled.

'You're never looking at my feet,' Donald smiled back.

There was a silent pause as Donald looked at Brendon gratefully. 'I really want to thank you, mate, for bringing me here.' The words were genuine and heartfelt. 'I can't think of a better guide or friend. It feels just great being together, doesn't it? Like we've been friends forever.'

'Maybe we have,' Brendon replied. 'Soul mates, eh?'

That night, after a delicious dinner, they wandered the cobbled streets and found themselves unexpectedly at the beautiful Trevi Fountain, illuminated by floodlights: the place for lovers. Mesmerised, they sat on one of the benches amidst a crowd of tourists and lovers.

After a few moments and affected by the location and the other couples sitting and standing nearby, some licking gelati, some murmuring quietly, some kissing, Brendon attempted a little history to distract them from the ambience.

'You know, hundreds of years ago in Ancient Rome, this used to be a major aqueduct that supplied drinking water to the populace. You can actually see the representation of the Roman technicians locating the source of the spring of pure water on the facade there,' he said, pointing. 'The aqueduct was originally over twenty kilometres long and led the water all the way to the Baths of Agrippa until the Goths attacked Rome and cut off the water supply and the locals had to get their water from polluted wells and the Tiber River, which also wasn't all that clean. Anyway, hundreds of years later this was designed by a bloke named Nicola Salvi which wasn't all that popular at the time because he was from Florence and some of the Romans were really pissed off because there was a huge rivalry between the two camps but he built it anyway.

'Thank God he did,' Donald remarked. 'And who's the big stone bloke in the middle?'

'Do you really want to know?' Brendon asked with a smile.

Donald nodded.

'Pietro Bracci's Oceanus,' Brendon announced and then laughed at Donald's stupefied reaction.

'Oh, that guy!' Donald said, as though he was familiar with the name. 'He used to play centre for the Warrego Wanderers, right?'

'Yep, that's the guy,' Brendon laughed. 'Didn't he drown in the surf at Portsea?'

'No you dork, that was Harold Holt,' Donald replied knowledgeably.

'Anyway, poor old Salvi died before it was finished,' Brendon went on to finish the story, 'and a bloke called Giuseppe Pannini took over. The funny thing was that there was a barber's pole in the original design for some reason and Pannini hated it and moved to behind that sculpture over there,' he said pointing to a sculpted vase. 'The Romans call it the Ace of Cups.'

'Speaking of cups,' Donald said, 'How about we head back to the hotel for a nightcap before we turn in? I'm beginning to feel beat and I'm not sure if it's the jetlag or architectural overload.'

'Good idea,' Brendon said, standing. 'I'm getting a bit tired of statues of naked men, I think I'm ready for a bit of real Mc Coy.'

That night by unspoken mutual consent their passion and relationship moved to another level and they were replete. The next morning Brendon was able to meditate properly for the first time since meeting Donald.

Chapter 13

Donald stood in middle of the Forum in awe as Brendon pointed out the various ruins that littered the place.

'My God!' he exclaimed, 'this is magnificent!'

Brendon, having seen the place on a previous visit in his gap year before University, laughed at Donald's astonishment. 'And do you know where you're standing right now?' he asked

Donald looked down at the stone platform he was standing on and shook his head.

'You are standing on what is called the New Rostra and that is where the orators stood to address the plebs. As a matter of fact that is exactly where Marc Anthony stood to give his oration over Julius Caesar's body.'

'You're joking,' Donald responded in amazement.

Brendon shook his head. 'Only you're facing the wrong way. You would've been speaking to the Senators. That's how they used to make their addresses but when Rome became a Republic after Caesar got the point, so to speak; several points, in fact, it was considered the orators should face the general populace instead. So, I guess Marc Anthony would've faced that way,' he said, indicating.

'Friends, Romans, Countrymen…' Donald began to recite the speech from Shakespeare's famous play but Brendon placed his hands over his ears.

'No, no, no!' he said loud enough to interrupt Donald's oration. 'Do you know how many tourists have done that? Probably thousands over the years.'

'Sorry,' Donald said, 'I just couldn't resist it.'

'Try,' Brendon suggested dryly, 'or beware the ides of October,' he warned him, intentionally misquoting the original. 'And just over there is where they burnt Caesar's body,' he continued, ignoring Donald's interruption.

'And you said before the senate was just over there?' Donald said pointing. Brendon nodded. 'Well, that's not far, they could've dragged him over here, save the hearse driver.'

'Ah, but he wasn't killed outside the Senate, or the Curia Julia, as it was then called, it was being renovated so the Senate was meeting at the Theatre of Pompey, a few blocks up the road. Brutus, Cassius and his mob jumped him outside there. And besides, there was all the pomp and ceremony of the funeral procession before they could actually torch his Toga, so to speak.'

Donald stood looking around trying to imagine what it must've been like over two thousand years ago with the parades and victory marches, the colour, smells and noise of the jostling disparate crowds. He knew that Rome had been a very cosmopolitan city made up of maybe hundreds of different races and tribes who were attracted to the centre of the known world. He remembered Brendon pointing out the marker that was considered the centre of Rome signifying that was where 'all roads led to'.

He got off the Rostra and sat on a nearby rock, slipping into a reverie that he could feel in his bones and he could almost envision the scene as it must've been thousands of years ago. He could ignore the dozens of tourists milling around the ruins and the constant archaeological diggings going on all over the place, they didn't disturb him but eventually Brendon's voice calling him from a short distance away, did.

'Hey, Donald, let's go over and take a look at the arch of Septimius Severus, it's a masterpiece of carving and construction.

Donald rose to his feet and followed, gradually catching up with him where Brendon continued the history lesson.

'This magnificent, crumbling piece of work was built to commemorate the victories of Emperor Septimius Severus over the Parthians,' he lectured, almost like one of the tour guides they'd unobtrusively followed until they were caught out and nonchalantly meandered off, lagging behind the group but still managing to catch the odd bit of commentary on the ruins. They'd heard the lectures on the Forum main Square, the Temple of Castor and Pollux and the Temples of Vesta and Saturn, which saved Brendon having to explain too much of the history of the ruins that still remained. He was more interested in watching Donald's incredulous expressions and the realisation that there were so many layers of past glories lying deep below their feet because the early Romans had a habit of just building one edifice on top of the other: an archaeologist's ultimate wet dream really because the whole forum was originally built on a swamp.

'Okay, teach, time for lunch,' Donald remarked, calling a halt, his brain and feet aching from information overload and all the walking. 'Let's eat.'

'Right,' said Brendon decisively, 'the Capitoline Museum restaurant it is. Come on, get a move on, we've still got the Coliseum to do this afternoon.'

'I hope it's licensed, I need a beer,' Donald groaned, as he followed.

'Where's the big, butch, star footballer who can run the field for twenty minutes without puffing?' Brendon laughed as he led the way.

'I'm only good for short bursts not for fucking hours on the run,' Donald replied, in his defence.

'Now, this is more like it,' Donald said as he sank into the armchair at the rooftop restaurant table, which overlooked the forum in all its ancient glory with an ice cold beer at his elbow and another on standby as a chaser.

'Well, what's your reaction so far?' Brendon asked also sipping at his pre luncheon Campari.

'Fantastic,' Donald exclaimed, 'it must've been the biggest recycling yard in the world. What happened to all the rest of the rubble?'

'Well, actually you're right,' Brendon replied, indicating the Forum far below. 'Over the centuries it slowly got covered in at least thirty feet of rubble and soil. In fact in the Middle Ages it was used to graze sheep and cattle and no one knew or cared about the archaeological treasures underneath. As the Forum fell into disrepair there were tons of marble, stone and works of art removed and mostly lost to posterity to use for other buildings, palaces and churches and even ordinary homes. It was like a huge hardware store only you didn't have to pay for the stuff you pinched in most cases. It was just lying there, unused, so why not use it?'

'Why not indeed,' Donald agreed. 'It would make a great outdoor dunny.'

'As you probably know, the Coliseum over there,' Brendon indicated, which really wasn't necessary, it being in full view, 'where we're heading after lunch…' Donald groaned but Brendon persisted, 'was originally covered in white marble, which must've been spectacular but when Napoleon arrived to do a bit of plundering, raping and pillaging, they pulled the marble off so they could use the iron cleats for cannon and ammunition.'

'Waste not, want not,' was Donald's practical response.

'You ignorant plebeian,' Brendon commented, disdainfully. 'I really don't know what attracted me to you.'

'I do,' Donald replied suggestively, 'my brain.'

'Well, I can't think of anything else,' Brendon laughed.

There was a pause in the conversation as they ate their preferred antipasto and took in the view, comfortable together in their silence.

'Tell me,' Brendon finally broke their contemplation, 'did you get any feeling or even the slightest inkling as you wandered around down there that you might've been there before?'

Donald tore his gaze away from the spectacular view and groaned. 'Here we go again. Do you think I'm a reincarnated Marc Anthony just because I happened to stand on that stage?'

'Rostrum,' Brendon said, correcting him.

'Okay, *rostrum,*' Donald accepted the correction. 'I think it's pretty certain that everybody escapes into their imagination when you're surrounded by such a colourful and historic place. Why, did you imagine yourself in a toga, lying back on a cushion being fed grapes by Linda?'

Brendon shrugged. 'I've been here before a few times but I must admit on my very first visit, I felt a sort of familiarity.

'Maybe your overactive imagination,' Donald responded.

'Maybe,' Brendon replied, thoughtfully.

The difference was immediate as soon as Donald walked into the Coliseum. He felt a sudden quickening of his heartbeat exactly as he felt before entering a football stadium. Brendon instantly noticed his sudden change. Donald was simply standing transfixed on a platform that'd been built to represent part he original ground level when combat and bloodshed had dominated the arena. His gaze took in the ruins of the subterranean cells below where the gladiators, animals and wretched victims were held before they entered for mortal combat and terrible deaths. Although the October weather was clear and warm, he shivered.

'You okay?' Brendon asked.

Donald seemed to shake himself free of the uncomfortable mood and smiled at his friend.

'Yeah, I'm fine but…'

'But what?' Brendon asked curiously.

'I think I have been here before,' Donald replied dreamily as the feeling seemed to persist, 'as a combatant, not a spectator,' he continued, as he appeared once more to drift off into a reverie. 'I can see men fighting to the death, wild animals, wild men, fighting and killing each other in combat, blood gushing, limbs and heads falling to the ground, crowds of drunken spectators yelling from the tiers of seating, all yelling for blood, some retching over the people in front of them.' He turned and looked seriously at Brendon. 'I think it was the 2010 finals at the MCG.'

Brendon cuffed him across the back of the head. Donald collapsed in laughter having fooled Brendon into believing he was re-visiting another incarnation.

Chapter 14

By comparison to the previous day, the difference was immeasurable. They stood inside the foyer of St Peter's Basilica and the silence, reverence and opulence was palpable.

'My God,' exclaimed Donald in a whisper that fully described his immediate reaction.

'If you're going to pray you'd better kneel down and kiss my ring,' Brendon whispered irreverently back to him, the liturgical atmosphere making it impossible to raise his voice.

'No, I mean just look at the wealth and art,' Donald marvelled. 'We're surrounded with priceless works of art and architecture; no wonder people are overawed with religion. What do you think this artwork would be worth? I mean, there's millions of dollars on display and think of the poor and starving followers who helped pay for it.'

'Ah,' Brendon whispered back as he also cast his eye around the ostentatious surroundings, 'but, if the Church hadn't been this wealthy, think of the priceless works of art the world would've missed out on. Everything has its price, my heretic friend.'

Donald shook his head in denial and Brendon took him by the arm and led him to his right to an incredibly beautiful sculpture enclosed in bullet proof glass.

'This is one of the particular pieces I wanted you to see, The Pieta.'

'Michelangelo,' Donald immediately responded in awe. 'I've seen pictures of it. You see, I'm not that ignorant.'

'No, the one thing I wouldn't call you is ignorant,' Brendon smiled.

'What was the name of the bloke who attacked it with a hammer,' Donald asked, remembering reading about it in a book.

'Toth,' Brendon answered. 'A nutter who thought he was the reincarnation of Jesus. He hit it fifteen times with a sculptor's hammer: knocked Mary's arm off at the elbow, a chunk off her nose and chipped one of her eyelids before he was finally subdued, by an American sculptor and a few others by the way. Funny thing, though, he wasn't ever charged. He was locked up in a nuthouse for a couple of years and then deported back to Australia and they stuck him in a nursing home in Strathfield, would you believe? And you wonder why Australian tourists have such a bad name.'

'It's been beautifully restored though,' Donald said, leaning in for a closer look. 'You can't even tell it was damaged.'

'Yeah, they did a great job with it,' Brendon agreed. 'It's still considered one of the greatest pieces of sculpture in the world.'

'It is incredibly remarkable,' Donald responded, studying the magnificent piece of marble sculpture, 'but don't you think Mary looks a bit young to be the mother of a thirty-year-old son?'

Brendon chuckled quietly. 'A lot of people say that but Michelangelo reckoned that Mary was so pure and unsullied that she never would've shown her age. Bit like you, really,' he joked. Donald gave him a wry look but Brendon continued, 'If you look very closely you'll see Michelangelo actually carved his name on Mary's sash: it was the only piece of his work he ever signed because some of his critics claimed it was actually carved by one of Michelangelo's competitors, a bloke by the name of Il Gobbo, so Michelangelo put a stop to that rumour in no uncertain terms.'

'It makes you feel you should convert to Catholicism, doesn't it?' Donald whispered.

'I think that was the idea,' Brendon whispered back, 'and the opportunity for a lot of greed. I try to forget the religious aspect and concentrate on the craftsmanship. It really knocks my socks off. I always feel a sense of belonging, somehow; the renaissance period really strikes a chord with me. That's why I bought you here to see if you felt the same connection.'

'I don't think so,' replied Donald, thoughtfully. 'I mean, I can appreciate the beauty and art of the place but I don't feel drawn to it in any way, repulsed if anything by the ostentation.'

Brendon almost looked disappointed. Deep inside he felt that maybe this was the connection he felt with Donald; maybe as an artist and model or pupil from the Renaissance period like the love and attraction the tortured Michelangelo and Leonardo Da Vinci and many other famous artists felt for their friends and lovers. Pushing the disappointment away he said, 'Let's take a look at the Sistine Chapel before lunch. Michelangelo helped designed the whole Basilica, as you probably know, but the Sistine Chapel ceiling is one of the few actual paintings he did. He preferred sculpturing. Most of the cartoons or designs he did of his work have disappeared but the chapel ceiling remains and shows what a fabulous artist he really was. It overwhelms me every time I see it. It's funny that he apparently didn't want to do it and probably hated every minute of it and yet it remains one of the world's greatest works of art.'

'Do you ever feel the same way about your work,' Donald asked curiously. 'I mean have you ever hated doing any of your work?'

Brendon hesitated before he answered and thought back to several instances. 'Sometimes,' he considered, 'when I feel I'm missing a certain aspect I want to portray or feel the colour isn't exactly as I want it. I've often painted the whole work out and started again from scratch. It's not unusual, to coin a phrase or a song title.'

'Really?' Donald replied in disbelief. 'You always seemed so sure of yourself when you were painting me. You worked so quickly and confidently.'

'That's because you inspired me almost from the first moment I saw you,' Brendon replied, sincerely. 'I knew what I wanted to achieve with you.'

'And you did – in more ways than one,' Donald replied, mischievously.

The Sistine Chapel had the desired effect on Donald and he was stunned into silence at the magnificence which was just as well as the Papal security guards kept a strict lookout on the thousands of tourists drawn to this iconic work of art and continually quietened the enthralled viewers and prohibited the many who wanted to lie on the floor and look up to admire the incredible fresco. Brendon was once again fascinated with the craftsmanship and sheer beauty of the work which had taken Michelangelo over four years to complete and for which the artist had received very little in the way of payment as his patron, Pope Julius the second, or, '*Il papa terribile*', as he was known, kept delaying payments to the maestro with the promise of future works for which he was promised he would be well paid. He had several works already in progress including that of the Pope's tomb which was never finished and for which he received very little in recompense for the expenses of materials Michelangelo had to pay for out of his own pocket. Artists are so desperate to have their work displayed and admired they sometimes ignore the material necessities of life, like eating.

'*Il papa* was a tight bastard,' Brendon announced to Donald, quietly, 'but then again, most of them were. 'An artist's lot is not always a profitable one,' he added.

'Well, you didn't do so badly out of your exhibition,' Donald reminded him.

Brendon shrugged. 'Well, some of us have smarter agents who are better businessmen than others but I doubt mine will last as long as this, or be as memorable.'

Afterwards, as Brendon and Donald enjoyed a cup of coffee at a nearby trattoria with a meal of spaghetti alla carbonara, a dish that had originated in Rome, they discussed the brilliance of the work and the artist.

'Michelangelo didn't approve of bathing, you know, a quick wipe over with a rag was good enough for him,' he informed Donald. 'He thought immersing yourself in water was bad for your health. That was a common belief in those days.'

'I'll bet that went over big with his boyfriends,' Donald replied, with a grimace, 'I hope he kept up a good supply of Eau Savage.'

'Probably Eau Arno, he was from Florence,' Brendon replied, with a laugh. 'It was a marvellous feat though; five thousand square feet of brilliance and pretty well all done with his left hand; he was a lefty. He had a little help from his apprentices but only the unimportant parts like bits of the sky and the odd unimportant figures and of course mixing the plaster and paints for the day's work. He worked like a madman. Frescos have to be painted on wet plaster or they won't stick. Da Vinci had that problem with The Last Supper; the plaster drying out or mould forming was a big problem.

'Da Vinci was gay too, wasn't he?' Donald asked.

'Yep,' Brendon replied, casually. 'He was renowned for dipping his brush in other blokes' pots, Gian Giacomo Caprotti da Oreno, or Salai, as he was nicknamed, and Count Francesco Melzi to name just a few. Salai was a right little mongrel too; he was a thief and a prostitute but was referred to as, not uncommonly at the time, a "model". He ripped Leonardo off something terrible so he was obviously a good fuck. Sodomy was a serious crime by that time in Florence, punishable by death if they caught you at it,' Brendon informed him, wagging a warning finger in Donald's face, jokingly. 'The Church decided not to agree with it even though it was pretty prevalent and still is and always will be. They thought there was so much of it going on that it would affect the population growth,' he laughed, 'But, even if they got married and had children it was still not unusual for the odd bit of "perversion" or "unacceptable sexual appetite", which was mostly ignored or covered up by the Church and political wankers anyway. It just went out of favour and became "un-natural", after going on for thousands of years,' he related contemptuously. 'Oh, well, fashions come and fashions go, but sexual appetite goes on forever amongst the young,' he lamented, philosophically.

Chapter 15

For the next couple of days, Brendon dragged Donald around the cobbled streets and the various sites of Rome like a frenetic tourist guide. Donald was more than amenable; excited and interested in them all including the Piazza del Pantheon and the Piazza Navona, which Brendon schoolmasterly lectured him had once been the city market in the fifteenth century and then later transformed into a significant example of Baroque Roman architecture for Pope Innocent the Tenth's family palace which faced onto the piazza. He loved the Bernini fountains, the Fontana dei Quattro or the Fountain of Four Rivers and the Fontana del Moro with the statues of four Tritons and the statue of an African Moor wrestling with a dolphin and the Fountain of Neptune featuring the wondrous sea god, the work of Antonio Della Bitta in the latter part of the nineteenth century.

Brendon also pointed out the statue of Pasquino where Romans could leave vulgar and abusive messages of social comment which Donald suggested was sort of an historical version of the Domain in Hyde Park in Sydney where people could lecture and lampoon the politicians and the assembly and which was also, no doubt, also attended by the equivalent of the Federal Police and ASIO for a record of dissidents.

'Spies and suspected terrorists and trouble makers have always abounded in every city in the world,' Brendon commented, 'and have since time began. Somebody's got to keep an eye on them. They also used to flood this place when it was much lower every Saturday and Sunday in August for elaborate naval celebrations' and then they raised the pavement again in the nineteenth century and the market moved back in again and then out again in the late nineteenth century to the Campo De' Fiori.

'Market to market: couldn't make up their minds, eh?' said Donald.

'The Italians are always on the move,' Brendon said.

They staggered up the Spanish Steps, in the Piazza di Spagna, one of the world's most famous images and inspected the Barcaccia Fountain at its base. 'The last time I was at the Spanish steps,' Brendon said, 'it was in May and the steps were completely covered in pots of azaleas in brilliant colours. It was magnificent. Now it looks like, well, a set of stairs, but a beautiful set of stairs, spread out like a butterfly. People used to sit here and eat their lunch but that's been stopped now. I suppose the local *trattorias* complained. They want the tourists inside their establishments. And speaking of which, let's have a nice cup of tea at the famous Babington's Tea Rooms, off the Piazza. It opened in 1896 for the visiting English tourists who demanded their cuppa and it's still going strong. This used to be a very bohemian area once and now it's still a favourite meeting place but not quite so bohemian. Lord Byron, Percy Bysshe Shelley, Leigh Hunt, and Joseph Severn used to hang out here too.'

'Oh, we're in good company then,' Donald said, without recognising Hunt and Severn, 'poets, an artist and a footballer.'

Brendon nodded, missing the connection and also pointed out John Keats House, a building at the foot of the steps where the consumptive poet lived for a couple of years and finally died there and which was now The Keats-Shelley Memorial House but they decided against a tour as a good cup of tea had more appeal at that stage.

They cruised the Via del Corso with its myriad of exclusive shops and Donald was fascinated to see how ancient ruins turned up in the most unexpected spots of the city attached to modern buildings and streets. Brendon insisted they visit art galleries and watched Donald for any sign of familiarity with the paintings or locales they visited but to his disappointment there was little, if any, obvious cognitive response.

Nevertheless, despite Donald's protests, Brendon insisted that Donald should see the wondrous statue of Moses and off they trundled at a quick pace to the church of San Pietro in Vincoli. Donald was immediately impressed at the larger than life sculpture and particularly Moses' wonderfully flowing beard and the excellence of the anatomy, of which, Michelangelo was an undisputed expert, having studied anatomy diligently in his early years. But the beard fascinated Donald and wondered how such a flowing sense could possibly be achieved in marble.

'Are you sure he didn't do this with a brush in wet cement?' he asked Brendon, 'you can see almost every strand of hair and curl. It seems impossible that he could achieve that effect with a chisel.'

'Ever tried painting with marble dust?' Brendon replied sarcastically. 'No, the man was a pure genius with the chisel. But his paintings of women looked like they were Amazonian or paintings of men with female breasts; – very butch bodies.'

'But why the horns,' Donald asked quizzically, referring back to the Moses sculpture. 'Why would Moses have horns?'

Brendon smiled. 'That is open to more speculation than you can poke a stick at,' he replied, 'some say it was from a wrongly translated passage from Exodus in the Bible that was translated from the original Hebrew into Latin, about when Moses came down from Mount Sinai the second time with the new Commandments. God knows what happened to the first lot of Commandments but I don't think any of them stipulated it was a sin for a man to lie with another man,' he chuckled, 'I reckon that was added later when the theologians got hold of the Bible and added it to keep the deviates in line. They were prone to do that in the Renaissance period, certainly not from lack of opportunity.'

Despite the crowd of tourists, Donald laughed and several turned to glare at his irreligious heresy in such a Holy place which made Brendon convulse with laughter even louder than Donald. He controlled himself to continue in **a** more reverent tone, 'There's also been a lot of dispute about the glaring expression on Moses' face, his body language and the true meaning behind the work. Even Sigmund Freud spent a few weeks trying to work out the emotional truth behind Michelangelo's brilliant effect but even he couldn't explain it satisfactorily for everyone. He probably blamed Michelangelo's mother who was apparently a bit of a shrew. As for me, I don't really care. It talks to me of anger at the masses who insisted on defying God's words and he was not a happy chappie. The magic is in the craftsmanship – the genius.

He looked around at the rapt attention of the viewers and nudged Donald.

'It's a very important relic for the Jewish people,' he said, as he indicated a group of Orthodox Jews at the back of the crowd; black, black, black, clothes, hair, beards, hats, all standing together, rocking back and forward on their feet and quietly praying as if they were facing the Wailing Wall in Jerusalem. Both Brendon and Donald, without verbal agreement, left the church and the heavy atmosphere it was producing.

'Why do some religions all wear the same clothes?' Donald wondered. 'Is it to stand out and say, 'We're different, pay attention?'

'I think it's just so they can recognise their own,' Brendon replied, lightly. 'That way you don't get

Jews mixing with Muslims or Hare Krishnas. People love to stay in their groups. It gives them the feeling of belonging. Individuality is a dangerous thing.'

'Well, you could hardly miss each other in that get-up,' Donald replied, as they made their way down the steep hill towards their third coffee for the day.

'Well, tomorrow we're off to Florence,' Brendon said to Donald over his cup, 'You'll love it except for the million-odd tourists that congregate there almost all year round. It's been ranked as one of the most beautiful cities in the world and one of the biggest tourist drawcards. But you can almost ignore the tourists when you look at the brilliant architecture and works of art. The atmosphere in itself is captivating,' he raved, 'very different to Rome – gentler, somehow.'

'But I love Rome,' Donald exclaimed. 'This is a wonderfully busy and exciting place.'

Brendon sipped his coffee, pausing for thought. 'And did you feel any sort of attachment to it?'

'You mean do I think I once belonged here?' Donald sighed correctly guessing the inference behind Brendon's words. 'Sorry, I don't think so. There hasn't been any feeling of familiarity. Let's face it; it isn't hard to let your imagination fly off with your emotions, is it?'

'So, no feelings of familiarity with Rome at all?'

Donald thought, trying to recall his reactions to the beauty of the art works and the places he had seen. 'No, but they were incredibly impressive. But I have to admit, some of them left me a bit cold but I don't think that's the sort of reaction you're looking for.' Brendon looked disappointed. 'Sorry, mate, I guess I'm a bit of a washout, eh?'

'No, no,' Brendon reassured him, 'it's just that I feel particularly attracted to the Renaissance period and I thought maybe…'

'We'd been together there at some time, maybe as an artist and model or had a strong relationship then?' Donald finished the sentence for him. A sudden realisation hit him, 'Michelangelo? Did you think you were once Michelangelo?' he stifled a laugh.

Brendon had the good grace to be mortified with embarrassment at this suggestion, although anything was possible in the theory of Reincarnation where it is likely a soul brings with him certain strong traits from other incarnations. With a derisory laugh, he replied, 'No, of course not. Anyway he was mainly a sculptor, I'm a painter: and nowhere in the league of

Michelangelo. But I hoped we may have worked in his studio with him or another Renaissance artist or maybe had helped with his designs or acted as assistants,' he finished lamely. 'I just feel a great kinship to his work, that's all.'

Donald could restrain himself no longer and burst into uncontrollable laughter, much to Brendon's embarrassment. Finally controlling his outburst he said earnestly, 'Listen mate, you are an excellent artist; maybe even a great artist after you die, but a Michelangelo you ain't, even if you do knock off your models. I can just see you lying on your back painting the Sistine Chapel ceiling sucking off one of the assistants.'

'As a matter of fact, he didn't lie on his back to paint the ceiling,' Brendon corrected him. 'He had scaffolding built and stood on that and bent his head up.: Caused him no end of neck trouble for almost the rest of his life. You've been watching too many re-runs of Charlton Heston's movie: never happened.'

'Oh, now you're a movie expert as well?' Donald laughed.

'Okay,' Brendon relented, 'no more Renaissance art but that's going to be pretty hard in Florence, which was the heart of the Renaissance period. But

I'm sure we can find a night club or Gothic strip club or a decent bar so you can get pissed while I indulge myself.'

'Now you're talking,' replied Donald with a laugh.

'But there is one more piece of Michelangelo's work you must see; the statue of David, at the Academia. I promise you you'll be impressed.'

'Wouldn't miss it for the world,' Donald replied, 'It was on my bucket list, anyway. But do I really have to do the Uffizi? I'm just about out with wandering the halls of art galleries. '

'I wonder if we should go on to Athens,' Brendon suddenly remarked thoughtfully, 'I mean, with your boyhood experience in that exhibition you told me about and that sudden vision I had of you in the restaurant as a statue of a Greek god, it could be a clue.'

Donald rolled his eyes in incredulity at Brendon's persistence, 'How about we just enjoy each others' company and leave reincarnation to the Buddhists and Hindus?'

'And over half the world's population,' Brendon reminded him. And then, remembering Florence he suddenly said, 'And we've got to see some Leonardo da Vincis in Florence. He was a hometown boy who made good and he had relationships with quite a few of his pupils and Count Francesco Melzi, which were a bit suss.'

'My God, now he thinks he might've been da Vinci,' Donald exclaimed in disbelief as he let his head drop onto the coffee table.

Chapter 16

Florence was as wonderful as Brendon had described it – endlessly.

Donald was a bit surprised at first by the shabby neighbourhood around the train station but Brendon reminded him that all big cities had their slum or downtrodden areas and promised the old city, where they would be staying, would more than make up for the squalor of the more recent suburbs on the outskirts.

The relatively newly established Hotel, Firenz Number 9, on Via dei Conti, was a marvellous choice made even better by the inclusion of a small gymnasium and swimming pool and a view of the Duomo from their window. It was in the centre of the old city with ridiculously short walks to the major attractions and restaurants. Their double room was almost luxurious with parquet flooring in pale timber and had a marble bathroom, desk, wardrobes and the ceiling was actually frescoed in beautiful classical pattern. The bed was huge with an enormous white padded bed head. The Academia, which housed the world famous sculpture of David was only a few metres around the corner and Donald was eager to explore it before Brendon dragged him off to the several art galleries.

Donald had to agree Florence had a completely different atmosphere to Rome; more gracious and despite the tourists, even more fascinating with its ancient medieval charm devoid of the noisy traffic of Rome. He took to it immediately and this time it was he who dragged Brendon around discovering the wonderful Piazzas and sites and devouring the excellent food. They decided to breakfast out from the very first morning and Donald was surprised to see how the early morning workers dropped into their local coffee shop, stood at the counter and drank their espresso, standing up at the counter, almost in one gulp and some followed with a chaser of Vodka. Well, that'll set 'em up for the day he thought. Well, If ya can't beat 'em, join 'em, he thought, ordering a vodka for both he and Brendon, who paled at the thought.

They wandered the street admiring the Duomo and the magnificent Piazza della Signoria, with one of the finest collection of outdoor statues in the world, including Hercules and Cacus and the breathtaking, Fountain of Neptune and a copy of David, each resting along the impressive Palazzo Vecchio building. They were all magnificent but a little weatherworn after five centuries of standing out in the weather and the inevitable pollution which only enhanced them. Close by, was the impressive Loggia dei Lanzi with another collection of brilliant statues including the famous, Rape of the Sabine Women and Ercole and Centaur and Perseus, which Donald hadn't heard of.

'That's not the original Michelangelo's David,' Brendon informed him. 'Wait until you see the original. This one is damned good but there's something special about the original: for one thing it's cleaner. Now, we're almost next door to the Uffizi Museum which is arguably the greatest art museum in the world, so why don't we…'

Donald, with tourist map in hand, forcibly dragged Brendon off to the Academia in via Orsanmichele. He looked at the long queue of tourists and groaned.

'When in Rome you do as the Romans do,' Brendon said, 'and wait, and when in Florence…'

'You wait even longer,' Donald answered.

They eventually reached the entrance and presented their tickets which Brendon had purchased online before they started on the trip so they didn't have to wait as long as those who hadn't pre-paid for their admission. Donald bounded up the stairs, closely followed by Brendon at a more leisurely pace and entered the hallowed domed portal and stopped dead in his tracks. There it was in front of him; the statue that he had seen hundreds of times in photos but he never imagined that seeing the original in polished white marble at close range would have such an effect on him. He was stunned by the beauty and size of the most recognisable image in the world; the David, by Michelangelo!

They were lucky as not many tourists had gathered at that stage and they had only a few silent spectators for company and their presence didn't intrude upon Donald and Brendon's appreciation.

Donald was still standing thunderstruck as Brendon came up and stood behind him.

'What did I tell you, incredibly beautiful, right?'

Donald could only nod dumbly as he studied the huge, seventeen feet, perfect statue. He slowly walked around the masterpiece taking in every detail, the perfect anatomy, the smoothness of the almost translucent marble, the intricate detail, the beautiful face and short curly hair, the bend in the left arm holding the slingshot. 'You're right, it's even more impressive than the copy in the Piazza della Signoria. It's...' but he was lost for words.

'A world masterpiece of beauty and form,' Brendon concluded for him. 'You know, it reminds me a lot of you. That's just as you looked before the whistle blew and the finals match began, without the slingshot of course. Michelangelo captured the look just before he went into battle with the Goliath. Look at the moral power and concentrated tension he captured in the face. See, it's just the way you look before a game.'

Donald dismissed the flattering remark and replied, 'More like you, I think. My hands aren't that big but my dick is bigger, proportionally, I mean,' he added.'

'And circumcised,' Brendon added with a smile.

'Who was the original model? Donald asked.

'Well, that's a bit of a mystery,' Brendon replied. 'The consensus of opinion seems to be there was no single model but a compilation of many. Michelangelo had a remarkable memory recall and imagination and he was an expert on anatomy so maybe he didn't need a single model. He probably also had the personal experience of many naked young men he's rumoured to have had it off with. Did you know he was actually arrested and tried for sodomy?' he added as an afterthought. 'He and three or four other friends were accused of having it off with one of his models, Salai, or the little devil, as he was known, they could've been hanged but they got off with the help of very influential friends, like the Medici mob. As I told you, sodomy was a capital offence at that stage in Florence but very few were ever actually hanged for it.

'He did several small clay models but he worked entirely from his imagination and instinct for the finished work,' he continued, on a roll. 'One story goes that one of his contemporaries thought the nose was too big and Michelangelo hoisted himself up the scaffold and pretended to chisel bits away but actually he'd grabbed a handful of marble dust and chips, pretended he was chipping away and dropped them down from the scaffold to make it look like he was altering it but in fact it was left untouched, just as he planned it. The bloke at the bottom said, "Ah, yes, that's much better",' Brendon laughed. 'You can fool some of the critics some of the time, and all of the people all of the time.

'Two years work at six golden florins a month plus material expenses, and coffee I suppose,' Brendon added from his repertoire of knowledge from his Arts degree. 'There was also a romantic rumour that he travelled to Carerra and chose the particular block of marble because he could see the statue inside but in fact he inherited the block from a bloke called Agostino in Florence who had roughly hacked out a version of David and made a mess of it so Michelangelo was commissioned to take over. He wasn't happy with the size of the block because he thought it would restrict him but, being the genius he was, he came up with this masterpiece. It is true he believed he was only chipping away at the excess marble to liberate the figure battling to get out.

'Which reminds me,' he suddenly remembered, 'did you notice the unfinished statues in the corridor on the way in?

'No, I didn't,' confessed Donald. 'All I noticed was this. It does sort of catch your eye, doesn't it?'

'These are what I particularly wanted you to see,' Brendon said. He turned away and led Donald back down the corridor to the collection of unfinished sculptures that are known as the Unfinished Slaves. On their left, Brendon stopped at an obviously unfinished sculpture entitled 'The Awakening Slave'. It looked like the partially finished magnificent male image was attempting to struggle out of the marble block that was imprisoning it, a titanic struggle for the soul to escape the bounds of physical reality.

Donald stood utterly transfixed with the image and his eyes moved to Brendon's in sudden realisation.

'That's what you did with my portrait!' he exclaimed in wonder. 'I mean, it's not the same figure, of course, but the idea behind it!'

Brendon smiled in satisfaction, 'That's what Clifford was getting at and that is one of the main reasons for us coming over here. I never thought of this piece of work when I was painting you; it just appeared in my mind when I saw you lying in bed asleep with the ruffled brown bedspread under you. But I think it means the same thing. I recognised your soul trying to escape into rebirth.'

Donald's gaze returned to 'The Awakening Slave' in awe as the two men appraised it in admiration and bewilderment. Suddenly they were interrupted by a low, deep, female voice almost in their ear. 'He's not as pretty as the original.'

Both men turned in surprise and were suddenly face to face with Stephanie and Roxy, the two nurses Brendon had used as models for his Persian portrait.

'Steph and Roxy!' Brendon exclaimed in shock. 'What the hell are you doing here? I haven't seen you since you modelled for me!' He shook his head in disbelief as Stephanie and Roxy laughed at their stunned expressions. 'You missed the opening of my exhibition,' he admonished them. 'I tried to get in touch with you with an invitation but you'd disappeared. Where the hell did you get to?'

'We're with the *Sans Frontières* medical aid group and were only back in Australia to renew our work visas, which took forever, and left soon after your exhibition opened but we did sneak in to see it before we left,' Roxy laughed. 'That's how we recognised you both,' she said looking at Donald. 'This has got to be your model for that incredible painting, I hope,' she said, eyeing Donald appreciatively. 'Congratulations, Brendon, it was a wonderful exhibition.'

'Well, thank you, it did pretty well, actually,' he said. 'Yes, this is Donald who modelled for me and as a matter of fact that's how we managed to be here, a sort of celebration. Donald,' he said introducing the two women, 'this is Roxy and Stephanie. This is amazing!' he repeated, unable to believe the coincidence. 'So,' he stammered, 'how do you happen to be here, I mean in Florence, if you're with an aid group? I mean, I don't think they need aid workers in Florence, unless your here to nurse exhausted tourists?'

'No,' Stephanie laughed, 'we're on a bit of R&R before we're going back to Turkey to help out with the Syrian refugees. There are thousands of them crossing the border into Turkey and things are a bit of a mess over there with rebel and Syrian Government attacks.'

'But isn't that a bit dangerous?' Donald underestimated.

'You could say that,' she smiled wryly.

'No matter where they send us it's dangerous,' Roxy replied, with a shrug. 'Almost as bad as Kings Cross on a Saturday night. But people need help and Turkey's better than Africa,' she grimaced. 'Poor old Mandela; he got rid of apartheid and now there are hardly any whites with any experience left in the Government: So much for equality of the races now they have whites living in ghettos. The place is a shambles.'

Their conversation was obviously disturbing the tourists who had come to silently view the art exhibits and they were receiving quite a few disapproving looks so Brendon suggested they move on to a bar for a celebratory drink.

'Seen one naked masterpiece, seen 'em all,' Roxy remarked philosophically, 'and my feet are killing me so I can't think of anything better.'

They left the museum and made their way to a bar the girls were familiar with and settled in for a few welcome drinks and a catch-up on each others' news.

Almost naturally, Brendon escorted Stephanie and Donald was only too pleased to accompany the beautiful Roxy.

Chapter 17

They crossed the Arno River at the Ponte Vecchio to a very fashionable bar called the La Terrazza and Donald had his first look at the Arno and was amazed at the crowds, jewellery and souvenir stalls that lined the bridge and was constantly being hassled by Roxy and the others to stop browsing and hurry up before they died of thirst and exhaustion. They found a roof top table and settled in for a chat and some serious drinking.

'We're actually based in Istanbul,' Roxy said, but we get choppered around the country where we're needed,' she said as their drinks arrived. 'Mostly we get sent to southern Turkey near the Syrian border because that's where most of the refugees are arriving: thousands of them. We drop off drug and medical supplies and dress wounds and help the doctors where we can and try to avoid getting raped by the security forces. Most of the refugees are young men and you know how women are treated in the Middle East. The conditions make it impossible to actually live in the refugee camps for any length of time, some are just plastic tents and even shipping containers and there are so many camps and refugees it's getting hard for the Government to keep it under control. We might stay for a couple of days in a camp and help out where we're needed and then fly back to Istanbul. It keeps us pretty busy.

'So why go there?' Donald asked, 'why Turkey?'

Roxy and Stephanie looked at each other and shrugged, 'we're both good nurses and that's what we do; help people who need us,' Stephanie replied, simply.

'But why Turkey,' Donald persisted, 'the entire Middle East is a powder keg; it's very dangerous.'

'Yes, so we've seen,' replied Roxy, glancing at her companion wryly, 'especially in the south. 'But we've travelled the Middle East extensively and we love it; the people are marvellous and it's historically a fascinating place. There having a pretty rough time there at the moment and we want to help.'

'The word "crazy" springs to mind,' Brendon cut in.

Both girls laughed and Stephanie raised her finger in the air and pointed at Roxy as if discovering a new word, 'Crazy! That's the word! I told you it wasn't "adventurous".'

'Now that's where you should be going,' Stephanie said to Brendon, 'Istanbul or anywhere in Turkey. It's a beautiful country. It would be an inspiration for your next exhibition. We could do a tour of the refugee camps and you could capture the faces of all the suffering. The babies and the children break your heart.'

'Just what I need,' Brendon replied wryly, 'a bit of suffering in my life.'

'And why not?' Stephanie replied. 'Makes you realise how lucky you are to live in Australia and how soft you've got it.'

'If I want Middle Eastern suffering I just head west of Sydney,' he replied.

They continued chatting about their travels and drinking more and more and laughing a lot but Donald had suddenly gone quiet as he stared out over the Arno River at the beautiful skyline of Florence.

Brendon noticed and said, 'I think it's time for the Uffizi. Donald looks like he's getting bored with the company.'

That startled Donald from his reverie and he recovered, wailing, 'Noooo, not another art gallery. Let me just stay here and drink myself into a stupor and fall into the Arno.'

Roxy spoke up in sympathy. 'Tell you what; I've seen the Uffizi so why don't you two take a tour and Donald and I will have a nice, quiet walk around and soak up the local colour? It sounds like he's due for some art downtime. And Stephanie is much more into art than I am. She even knows who Artemisia Gentileschi is.'

'Judith and Holophernes,' Brendon immediately interrupted, knowledgeably. 'One of the few women painters displayed in the Uffizi. Most famous women painters of the seventeenth century weren't taken seriously. She was the first female painter to become a member of the prestigious Accademia di Arti del Disegno here in Florence. She apparently was raped when she was a young woman and didn't like it so most of her paintings were dark and violent.'

'And,' Stephanie butted in, not to be outdone, 'the painting of Judith depicts her and her friend beheading an Assyrian bloke she'd seduced while still retaining her chastity and purity, as all good girls should do. She was very Women's Lib before her time. I've never seen the original though so we must have a look at that,' she said, turning to Brendon.

'And the Caravaggios, and Titians, and Botticellis, and…' he added enthusiastically.

'Okay, you two,' Roxy broke in, 'let's save the art class until over dinner, eh?' And then, pointing to the exit purposefully she ordered, 'Go!'

'Roxy, I love you,' Donald sighed in relief.

'I have that effect on all the young, good-looking AFL footballers' she smiled.

'How did you know I played AFL?' Donald asked in surprise.

'Are you mad? I was at the finals,' she remarked, coolly. 'You mean you didn't see me?'

Both Donald and Brendon were amazed. 'I'm a huge fan of the AFL,' she laughed.

'Okay, you artsy crafty pair,' Donald said, referring to Brendon and Stephanie, 'on your bikes, go look at the Old Masters and this beautiful young, intelligent lady and I will discuss the artistry of football.'

'Sounds good to me,' said Stephanie, laughing. 'I'm sick of her company anyway,' she said jokingly. 'I'm in the need of sensitive male company. What do you reckon, Brendon?'

'You're on,' he said and then turning to Roxy and Donald he said, 'How about we all meet up for dinner under Neptune's statue in the Piazza della Signoria, at about six-ish?'

Brendon stood in front of the captivating painting, lost in admiration and familiarity. He'd seen it before and it had always appealed to him in its glorious line and form.

'I thought you'd like this one,' Stephanie said, with a knowing smile playing around her lips. They were standing in front of Titian's beautiful study of womanhood, 'Venus of Urbino', in Brendon's opinion, one of the most beautiful and sensual paintings of a naked woman he had ever seen.

'I love the way he's kept her in centre field in light warm colours with the darkened background,' he said, 'and the clever inclusion of the maid and the little girl representing housewifely duties and the dog which is supposed to represent marriage, though God knows why. I suppose he's inferring it's a dog's life.'

Stephanie laughed and dug him in the ribs.

'To me she represents the perfect Renaissance woman,' he said wistfully, 'the symbol of love, beauty and desirability. I wish I'd had the chance to paint her.'

'Oh, Roxy and I weren't good enough for you?' she said in mock indignation.

'Oh yes, you two were perfect,' he assured her, instantly, 'but this one was given to the wife of a duke to remind her of her marital obligations to fulfil her husband's needs.' He added seductively, 'you two wouldn't be in it.'

'We weren't married and you didn't ask,' she replied, playfully.

'I inferred,' he said defensively.

'Times have changed and we girls are free to go after what we want, when we want it without depending on you men to support us or to make the first move so stick around, buddy, and you might get lucky,' she said as she walked away to view a Caravaggio.

Her words and Brendon's surprised reaction held a very real prospect of carnal implication and his mind flew back to the sexual excitement he felt when they had posed for him in his studio and the no-go zone they had stipulated before they agreed to pose for him. Was that just a subtle ruse that had passed over his head? Surely not. Should he have been more persuasive; insistent even? No, it was their choice, I gave them the chance and they knocked me back and left before I could convert a try, he thought. Donald would be ashamed of me.

'Here it is,' exclaimed Stephanie, 'Judith and Holophernes – Artemisia Gentileschi. I didn't know they had the original at the Uffizi. My God, her women were strong. I wonder if she was gay?'

'I don't think so,' Brendon replied, suddenly drawn to the painting of the Biblical Judith and a female friend severing the head of Holophernes. 'She was married and lived in Rome and Naples after she'd studied under her father and another painter called Agostino Tassi who finally got round to raping her. The funny thing is she finished up marrying Tassi even though she taken him to court for the rape and had him convicted. He'd promised her he'd marry her but then he shot through so she married a couple of other husbands and probably made their life hell. That's Italian women for you,' he laughed.

Stephanie walked on but for some strange reason, Brendon felt compelled to linger and study the work more closely. As far as he remembered he'd never seen the original before and somehow it fascinated him.

For a change, Donald wasn't thinking of Brendon. He and Roxy were having a wonderful time seeing the sights, drinking coffee and licking gelato as they idly wandered around Florence. She was excellent, intelligent company and he was stimulated by her nearness, beauty and personal warmth. They walked down the long tree lined colonnades in the Boboli Gardens without even considering going into the Pitti Palace. Donald had had enough of antiquity for the time being and a different inner urge was pushing its way into his consciousness; a more carnal one. Maybe I'm not entirely gay after all, he thought. Yep, bi-sexual for sure. Now, that's handy; the best of both worlds. I wouldn't mind rooting this lovely young lady at all. But, there'll always be Brendon for the masculine company I crave when I'm with him. My needs for him are different, more fulfilling somehow, like we are of one mind. I wonder how he'd feel about me getting off with Roxy, or any other woman, he wondered, he did say we always had a choice.

'So, what about your parents?' she was asking, breaking his train of thought, as they sat on the trimmed green lawn overlooking the magnificent Pitti Palace and gardens.

'What?' he said, his carnal thoughts interrupted, 'Oh, we have a cattle station in south-east Queensland,' he said off-handedly. 'Five thousand square miles. "Alexandria" it's called. Well, Mum has the cattle station now; my father died when the homestead burned down during the drought of the eighties. I was only a young kid. He got Mum and I out and went back in for her jewellery box. He didn't come back out.'

'Oh, that's terrible,' Roxy said, shocked. 'Every boy needs a father. And your mother still lives out there?'

Donald nodded with a rueful smile. 'Oh, yes, she has a manager, housekeeper and stockmen of course. She's a very strong lady. Land is everything to my family. They'll carry her off in a box.'

'So what about you? How come you became a football player?'

He shrugged. 'Mum wanted me to go out, get an education and a taste of city life and try my hand at something else before I settled back into the country life. I used to kick a ball around on the station with a few Aboriginal mates and played at University in Sydney and a scout picked me up. I'll go back to Alexandria when my football career finishes, I suppose, but I don't know yet. It's not an easy life on the land. We get hit with droughts for seasons on end and floods the next. We're close to Coopers Creek and a few tributaries,' he explained.

'What were you doing at Uni?' she asked.

'Economics and Ecology,' he replied. 'Got to keep ahead of the business when you're on the land. Mind you, I learned more about ecology and land management from the local tribe than I did at Uni,' he laughed.

'So, Brendon's your sort of father figure?'

Donald roared with laughter and lay back on the ground. 'No, I don't think he'd like to be called my father figure. I used to see him around at Uni but we were never close friends then. He was a couple of years ahead of me and he was into Visual Arts. We met up again at the gym. We're just good mates now, very good mates, we're always there for each other.'

'So you love him like a brother?' she asked.

Donald smiled, thinking of Brendon and what they meant to each other. 'Yes, I love him,' he said simply and then quickly turned the conversation before it got tricky. 'And what about you and Stephanie; you seem to be good mates?'

'Oh, yes,' she smiled, 'but we weren't always. We've had several fallouts over the years since we went to school together. But we do complement each other in many ways. It's like being sisters with the edge of rivalry that so many sisters have. We seem to have come to an understanding in recent years and respect each other. We wouldn't hurt each other for the world now but there was a time…' She left the rest unsaid.

'Let's start getting back,' he said holding out his hand to help her up. 'I wonder how the art class is coming along.'

'They're a good pair,' Roxy said. 'Steph is mad on art and I can take it or leave it.'

'But you know what you like?' he said, echoing Brendon's time-worn phrase.

'Yes, I do,' she said, holding out her hand for assistance and looking directly into his eyes.

The touch of her hand in his was comforting and vaguely familiar. Sorry, Brendon, he thought, I've got to have this one even for a night.

The same thought was going through Brendon's head about Stephanie and he too wondered what Donald would think about it. Well, he knows how I feel about free choice and no ties. He thought, but if it means hurting him or losing him, there's no contest. That man dwells inside of me, he thought. Two bodies, one soul.

Chapter 18

They dined at the Grand Hotel Baglioni on the Piazza Unita Italiana where the girls were staying and they weren't disappointed. The food, service and wine were excellent and their corner table was placed next to an expansive plate glass window that gave a wonderful view of the Duomo and the surrounding Florentine rooftops.

They chatted about their day; Stephanie and Brendon about the art treasures they'd seen at the Uffizi and Roxy and Donald about the marvels of the Bobili Gardens.

'The sculptures and fountains strewn all over the place are amazing,' Donald enthused, 'you would love them, Bren.'

'I did go through there a few years back,' Brendon replied, 'and I remember how blown away I was. Did you see the copy of Michelangelo's slaves in the grotto, like the ones we saw at the Academia?'

'Not as good as your version,' Donald replied with a conspiratorial smile as he finished his sweet course that was a work of art in itself.

But the conversation soon waned into more mundane subjects as the men questioned the girls about their lives in Istanbul. It was obvious they were very close and addicted to their work and again suggested that the two men should visit them while they were, 'in the neighbourhood'. They had a two bedroom apartment they would gladly share if Donald and Brendon decided to take them up on their offer.

Brendon and Donald shared a look whilst considering the idea and Brendon asked, 'How much longer are you on R&R?'

'We've got another week,' Roxy replied. 'We're off to Athens the day after tomorrow and then we'll fly back.'

'Oh, let's not talk about going back to work,' Stephanie grimaced and then replaced the look with a bright smile, 'why don't we have coffee and liqueur served in our room and we can relax and convince you to visit before you have to go back to Australia.'

'Well,' Brendon said, looking at Donald, 'you did say you wanted to see Greece, mate, so maybe we should take these two beautiful ladies up on their offer?'

'As long as I don't have to be forced to wander around anymore fucking art galleries,' Donald replied, sourly.

'Hey, I have an idea,' Brendon suddenly said, 'How about we fly to Athens with the girls and I'll hire a car and we can all drive to Istanbul together. It's only a few hours and we'll have the freedom to stop and maybe stay along the way if we want to. We'll be able to see more of the countryside and I promise, no more art galleries.' He stopped to gauge Donald's reaction and was pleased to see the excited change in his countenance.

'Sounds great to me,' he said, 'how about you girls? Want to risk a long road trip with two horny Aussie guys?'

Roxy and Stephanie shared that same questioning look that Brendon had captured in their portrait and then in obvious agreement they nodded to each other and shared a conspiratorial look that obviously included the prospect of rampant sex with these two gorgeous men.

The girls' room was not opulent but nicely decorated in cream and gold, quite large with a sofa and coffee table and easy chair in front of a sizeable window to take advantage of the view. A small writing desk and chair completed the furnishings.

There were two king-sized single beds, side by side against the wall. Room service delivered their order of coffee and a bottle of Cognac and the waiter departed without, to his credit, even the suggestion of suspicion of a forthcoming orgy showing on his face. They drank the coffee and sipped the warming brandy whilst they chattered about their forthcoming trip.

'Are you serious about flying to Athens and doing a road trip to Istanbul?' Roxy asked Brendon.

Brendon looked to Donald for his reaction and Donald grinned in approval. 'I'd love it,' he exclaimed, 'and maybe we could stop off at Anzac Cove on the way. We've got to see that.'

'Are you sure you have the time?' Brendon asked Roxy.

'Yes, of course,' she replied, 'we've actually done it in just over eight hours straight through so we can even stop along the way and make a few diversionary side trips if you like. We'll show you some of the more interesting spots. We call it our "Mini Alexander the Great" tour.

Donald's eyes brightened at the exciting prospect of following in the footsteps of one of the world's greatest conquerors and Brendon suddenly became intrigued.

'Tell you what,' he said, 'tomorrow, I'll arrange the flight to Athens and a hire car at the airport and we'll be on our way. We can fly back from Istanbul to Athens,' he said, turning to Donald. 'We can probably arrange for the car to be picked up in Istanbul if there's an office there, and we'll do Athens on the return trip. I have to show you around some of the museums in Athens,' he said, 'more art and history than you can poke a stick at.'

'Now why doesn't that surprise me?' Donald replied wryly.

Roxy rummaged in the room safe and found their airline tickets and wrote down the flight number they'd booked.

'See if you can get on the same flight,' she said as she handed the information to Brendon, 'it would be good if we can travel together. You can help us with our luggage,' she grinned.

Brendon folded the slip of paper and put it in his wallet. 'I'll get onto my laptop as soon as we get back to our hotel,' he said.

'You can organise tourist visas for Turkey on line, you know,' she said.

'I'll check it out,' he said.

After a couple more brandies, the girls excused themselves and both went into the bathroom leaving Brendon and Donald alone together.

'Why do girls always go to the toilet together?' Donald asked Brendon after they heard the bathroom door close.

'Why do you reckon?' Brendon quietly asked Donald the rhetorical question, 'to discuss their strategy I would suggest. It's pretty obvious what they have on their minds. You up for it or do you want to leave before the pubic hair hits the fan?'

'They are very rootable,' Donald whispered back in his usual forthright manner,' and a change might be as good as a holiday. I've never had a foursome.'

'Haven't you?' Brendon said in astonishment. 'Your sexual education is sadly lacking, my friend, but I think it's about to be expanded.'

'Did you bring condoms?' Donald whispered urgently.

'Tissues, Cialis, deodorant and condoms; part of my constant first aid kit,' Brendon replied, quickly slipping a couple of Cialis tablets from his pocket and handing one to Donald whilst swallowing the other with a gulp of brandy.

'Doubt if I'll need this,' Donald said, swallowing the tablet and there was a slight pause while he looked at Brendon dubiously, 'Do you think it will make any difference, to us I mean?' he asked tentatively.

Brendon smiled gently and kissed him lightly on the lips. 'Nothing and no-one will ever change the way I feel about you,' he said softly, 'but a bit of extra curricula experience may be a bit of fun. Now give us a hand with these beds,' he said, rising to push the two beds together.

They were interrupted by Roxy's voice from the bathroom, 'Okay, fellas, cover your eyes and no peeking until we tell you, okay?'

The men threw themselves back onto the couch and with a mutual glance at each other dutifully closed their eyes and waited for further instructions.

'Okay, now,' came the awaited instruction from Roxy and they opened their eyes.

Before them stood Roxy and Stephanie, completely naked, in exactly the same pose they had taken in Brendon's portrait of them. After the initial shock, both men collapsed in laughter.

'Now, let's take up where we left off,' said Stephanie with a seductive smile, 'the artist and his three bashful models, but this time you can paint us in melted chocolate.'

With that, Roxy advanced on Donald and Stephanie on Brendon, who stood eagerly awaiting the next development.

Each girl slowly began to undress their chosen partner as the men stood obediently, their ardour rising with each item of clothing being removed. First came their shirts, almost in unison, and the girls bent their heads to kiss their chests and softly nibble their nipples. The belts of their trousers were removed slowly but purposefully and the zips on their trousers opened to reveal their swelling manhood. Their slacks dropped to the floor, again almost in unison and the girls slid down their bodies, running their tongues down the boys' bodies on the way down, to retrieve their cast off clothes and throw them against the wall.

'Oh, fuck this,' Donald exploded and quickly removed his loafers and socks which joined the slacks on the floor with Brendon quickly following suit. Their now bulging briefs were the only clothing separating them from complete nakedness but the girls insisted on removing them, refusing the men's assistance, slowly kissing and running their tongues over the men's lower stomachs and finally down to their now well extended penises and testicles.'

Both men groaned in ecstasy and ran their hands over the girls' heads and through their long, lustrous hair. The girls stood and stepped back slowly raising their hands in invitation. The men moved forward and the two couples embraced, their hands exploring and caressing, their lips hungry and tongues searching and entwining for even greater heights of passion.

Without realising anything but their need for gratification in each other they found their way to the now king sized bed and sank onto it, locked in each other's embrace, they writhed and moaned in an erotic ballet of nakedness and lust, sharing their passion with each other and constantly changing partners to give and share the exquisite pleasure of sensual skin and willing impatient orifices.

All four were mindless of their fervour and were soon lost in the physical and vocal ecstasy of love making, giving and taking of each others' bodies without thought of who was sharing with whom.

Chapter 19

It seemed to Donald that the passion lasted through the entire night when in fact there were several breaks when they dozed, and recuperated their strength still entwined in each other's arms like a cluster of marble sculptures. He was aware that he and Brendon shared the middle of the bed, their naked bodies always in contact with each other which only added to the exquisite pleasure he felt. Roxy lay on the outside of him while Stephanie lay on the outside of Brendon and that is how they awoke in the morning.

There was no awkwardness between them and the memories of their sexual encounters stayed vividly in their minds. Eventually the girls rose from the bed, kissed their individual partners lightly and made their way to the bathroom where the men could hear the sound of the shower spraying over their bodies and the sounds of their voices laughing and obviously discussing the details of the evening's escapade.

'Wow,' Brendon said with a smile of satisfaction, 'what a double act. I'd say they've done that before.

It was almost choreographed. Was that good for you?'

Donald kissed him on the lips and returned the smile. 'Are you kidding? That was some of the most exciting sex I have ever had and I thought I'd had it all over the last few of months with you.' He sank back onto the pillows and stretched his magnificent body. Unable to resist, Brendon ran his hands lightly over Donald's body feeling the familiar strength and contours. 'Oh, not again,' Donald moaned in pleasure, 'I don't think the girls would appreciate us indulging ourselves without them.'

As if on cue the girls entered from the bathroom laughing. The men quickly drew apart and pulled the sheet over their lower nakedness.

'Oh, don't be coy, fellas,' Roxy laughed. 'I think we've seen everything there is to see. Now,' she continued in a businesslike tone as the girls started to dress, 'up you get and out of here, we girls have things to do. We'll meet you downstairs for breakfast if you like and then we have some shopping to do and you guys have our trip to plan.'

The men rolled out of bed, picked up their discarded clothes and headed for the bathroom to shower and dress.

'We'll meet you in the dining room so don't be long,' Stephanie called after them, 'I'm starving.'

'Order something for us,' called Donald, 'High protein.'

'We'll be down in a couple of shakes,' Brendon added from the bathroom.'

'No shaking in there,' Roxy called back, 'leave it to the experts.'

The shower was turned on and grabbing the soap, Donald and Brendon began to lather each other's bodies.

When their breakfast of toast, eggs, bacon, tomatoes and fruit followed by life saving coffee were demolished, Brendon and Donald said their farewells promising to keep the girls up to date on the trip and returned to their hotel.

They discussed the forthcoming trip with excitement and Brendon got to work on his laptop and organised tourist e-visas online and their plane tickets which he managed to book on the same flight as the girls. He also booked a car, complete with GPS, to be waiting for them at the Athens airport and on a roll he started researching a route for them to take. Everything was miraculously falling into place. Donald lay back on the bed and called out questions, answers and instructions. He felt the thrill and anticipation of exploring Greece and Turkey by car and several times Brendon had to tell him to shut up and stop interrupting him. Donald decided he should have one last look at Florence and left Brendon to his work agreeing to be back for lunch.

Donald wandered the crowded piazzas and back streets of the old city with a renewed vigour and eventually settled at an outdoor trattoria and ordered an espresso with a vodka chaser which he thought could well become a new habit. This gave him the chance to review the events of the trip to date and the expectations of the future.

The totally unexpected experience of meeting up with the girls and their sexual exploits of the previous evening were uppermost in his mind and he attempted to get the unbelievably exciting exploit into focus. It had been his first experience of what could only be described as a multiple sex orgy and he had to admit the effect on him had been staggering. The abandonment of his hitherto youthful principles of 'acceptable behaviour' was bewildering but he had been forearmed by his affair with Brendon which still puzzled him. He had opened sexual doors he hadn't imagined were possible for him and discovered areas of himself he never knew existed.

But he had to confront the fact that, although still confused, he felt a new inner sensation that thrilled him and felt preordained in some way. He was intent on discovering and exploring it to its fullest extent and to hell with the consequences.

Part of the confusion was his feelings towards Roxy who immediately attracted him to a similar extent to Brendon, but in no way as strongly. This was absolutely crazy as he had decided that Brendon had become the love of his life and he was more than content to embrace the abandonment of heterosexuality to Brendon's mysterious appeal. But the memory of Roxy's attractions with her glorious body and fascinating personality and appeal continued to haunt him until the two became as one in his mind. The more he thought about it, the more confused he became and he ordered another espresso and vodka; this time, doubles.

The unexpected involvement of the four disparate individuals, so far from his imagined future was too inconceivable to accept as an accident and he was forced to reconsider if Brendon's argument for reincarnation was in fact a possibility or was it just by chance that they had arrived at this point. They had all seemed to come together accidentally; first the rekindling of his and Brendon's past seemingly irrelevant relationship at University, which had taken a very unexpected turn into an enduring passion, the discovery of Roxy and Stephanie's portrait in Brendon's studio followed by their apparent 'accidental' meeting in Florence, miles away from home, the immediate attraction between the four of them which led to last night's incredible session of passion., which Donald had to admit, was more than just a sexual romp, and now their planned trip to Turkey together. Could it be possible that the four were somehow interrelated from the past to fulfil a reconciliation of some form? It was almost like they had all been set on some path to lead them to what destination?

He considered how Brendon had led him to reawaken his interest in reincarnation which he had held in his childhood but which had slowly lost impetus as he grew into manhood. He was certain that was what Brendon had in mind when he suggested this trip, ostensibly to Rome and Florence to discover if, together, they felt some connection to the Renaissance art period, which obviously fascinated Brendon but only left Donald impressed with the beauty and craftsmanship but not feeling spiritually connected in any way. But that appeared to have waned when no apparent re-awakening seemed to have occurred and they had relaxed into just enjoying each other's company and the pleasures of the trip.

His memory of the unfinished Michelangelo Sculptures of the Slaves stood out in his mind above all else with the similarity between them and the portrait Brendon had done of him and how the background had seemed to have changed without Brendon's interference. All of the images seemed to be trying to escape from their restraints but the background in Donald's portrait appeared to depict a legion of other figures trying to escape. Was that a secret symbol of what was happening to him? To escape his environs to rediscover a previous existence? To resolve past issues? Was he going completely mad thinking like this?

But the latest development with Roxy and Stephanie intrigued him. Where did they fit into the picture and what purpose, if any, would it serve? He and Brendon had never planned a car trip through Greece to Istanbul but because of Roxy and Stephanie they had succumbed to the idea willingly with little if any resistance and despite his many questions, the trip appealed to him enormously. The images of his childhood were lying hidden in the outskirts of his memory urging him to recognise them but there were still suspicion of an over active imagination being the cause of his present mental state.

Chapter 20

Because of Brendon's late booking and a relatively full plane load of passengers the two couples were seated separately which didn't particularly bother them and gave them the chance to read and talk. Donald didn't mention his confusion or excitement about the coming road trip and decided he would go with the flow and see what eventuated. Brendon sat beside him reading a book on Macedonia he'd picked up at the Florence Peretola airport book stand. They had an uneventful flight to Athens and arrived at the airport to go through the usual passport and customs maelstrom. Brendon then led the group to the car rental desk and received the keys and GPS he'd booked as they weren't kept in the cars for fear of theft. He was given directions and the location of the car and they proceeded to the exit. They found the car where the desk clerk had described. It was a brand new black Jeep Cherokee.

'You hired a Jeep?' Donald asked, copying a commercial he had seen on Television before he left Australia.

'Yep,' Brendon replied, with a self satisfied look that also mimicked the commercial, 'I hired a Jeep.'

'Well,' Roxy announced, bridging no argument, 'first rule is, I drive. The motorists in Greece are quite mad and rank with the worst in the world and I'm buggered if I'll put my life in the hands of a left side of the road Aussie driver, thank you. We've both done this trip a few times and we're now experts in surviving and we have a vague idea where we're going, so, keys please,' she said with authority, holding out her hand.

'Well, if you're going to be pushy about it,' Brendon said, surrendering the keys reluctantly. 'But I insist on sitting in the front passenger seat to keep an eye on you.'

'No, we don't move unless he sits up front with me,' she virtually demanded, indicating Donald.

'Stow the luggage in the boot, my good man' Donald said, as he smiled victoriously at Brendon and climbed into the front passenger seat.

'Okay you have a choice,' Roxy announced when they were all aboard, 'we can go straight through to Thessaloniki on the coast or head straight to Vergina in southern Macedonia.'

'I'll choose a vagina route every time,' Donald remarked.

'*Vergina*,' Roxy enunciated clearly. 'Anyway, from experience I think you'd take too long to arrive there. *Vergina*,' she over-enunciated again for his benefit, 'is close to a lot of wonderful archaeological sites I think you'll enjoy. It's near where Alexander the Great was born and his old man, King Philip 2nd, was murdered so you get two for the price of one.'

'Sounds great to me,' Donald said, 'a christening and a funeral all at the one time. Okay with you guys?' he turned and asked Brendon and Stephanie who were rather crowded together with extra luggage Brendon had thrown in the back seat. There was a grunt of mutual assent from the back seat and Roxy threw the car into drive and headed off at a speed that made Donald cringe and check his seatbelt.

'It will probably take us a couple of hours,' Roxy announced from the driver's seat as she swung to expertly avoid an oncoming truck and head for the freeway, 'depending on the bloody traffic on the motorway. If you're tired when we get there, we can always stay overnight and save the site seeing until tomorrow. There's a nice little hotel called the Aigon; it's actually in the Aiga area, very ancient, close to the ruins. We've stayed there before, lovely people run it and very helpful.' But Donald and

Brendon had their eyes shut tight in terror and didn't answer.

When they hit the motorway the three passengers relaxed and Donald and Brendon were able to take in the magnificent scenery they passed along the way.

'So we're heading into southern and then central Macedonia,' Roxy informed them. 'There's not an actual lot known about Alexander the Great's character but I think he was a power hungry nutter. This is where his conquests began. He was a very clever tactician and apparently had an amazing charisma but he also had the benefit of his father, Philip the second, who'd seized a pretty impressive empire of his own before Alexander arrived. Alexander managed to hold control over his Dad's empire as soon as his father had snuffed it and before any of the opposing warlords could take advantage of an empty throne. It was either hold back and be killed, which was the usual practice in those days when everybody was at war with everybody else, or get straight on your horse, take control of the army and start ruling the country and show everybody who was the boss. There's a strong suspicion his mother, Olympias, had Philip bumped off and maybe Alexander wasn't all that innocent either. Life was cheap in those days; it was all about power and control of the masses. Bit like a Hitler, I suppose.

'But he finished up ruling Greece in his own right, didn't he?' Brendon asked.

'Eventually,' Roxy replied, 'except Sparta, and after a lot of campaigning and slaughter and a fair bit of double dealing, which was an art of its own even in those days. You see, there were dozens of so called kingdoms all over Greece and his aim was to bring them all together under the one leader – himself – and collect all the booty along the way. It took him a couple of years of crossing the country back and forth subduing any opposition that arose and he knew he had to do it quickly or lose control. He was off on his rampages almost before the flames of his father's funeral pyre died down. To his credit, he succeeded and stabilised almost the whole country and a lot of his late father's conquests which of course included the wealth that he and Macedonia accumulated along the way.'

'You sound like you didn't like him very much,' Donald said.

She shrugged. 'He took what he wanted in return for their loyalty and their protection,' she said. 'Too much power and wealth inevitably corrupts. I'm a pacifist,' she added, 'that's why I try to help the disadvantaged.'

'But in those days surely it was better to have the protection of the army and a leader who was out for the Macedonians and Greeks,' he retorted with some mild hostility.

Roxy shrugged again. 'He gathered his armies from everywhere he conquered, not only Macedonians. He wasn't the least worried about who died for him and didn't give a toss for their wives and kids. There wasn't a lot that was all that wrong with the ruling Persian Empire he decimated,' she went on. 'They were fairly civilised for hundreds of years and brought a lot of beauty and science into their empire. Their king Darius was extremely just and wise for that period. But Alexander destroyed much of their culture and all their territory.'

'But hadn't Darius or his father invaded Macedonia years before?' Brendon asked.

'As I said,' Roxy re-stated patiently, 'Macedonia was a hotch-potch of tribes and different languages who were continuously fighting each other and Darius tried to bring them all together under the one ruler.'

'Him,' replied Donald disgustedly. 'So it came down to who had the biggest balls.'

'Basically, yes,' she replied, 'and from what I've read Alexander had a wonderful set.'

'So who has the biggest balls always wins,' Brendon concluded from the back seat.

'It's not the size, sweetie,' she said, 'it's what you do with them and with whom.'

They travelled on in silence for many miles, digesting Roxy's information and watching the scenery change and become hillier. Brendon and Donald became mesmerised by the scenery and sank into introversion.

Suddenly Stephanie spoke from the back seat, 'Roxy, why don't we call in on Aikaterine and Alexios on the way through?' and then turning to Donald and Brendon, she asked, 'Do you both ride? They have a wonderful property in the Balkan Hills with wonderful horses.'

'I told you I was from a cattle station,' Donald replied, 'so what do you think?'

'I'm an artist,' Brendon said, pompously, 'do they have a motorcycle?'

'They're friends we met in the aid corps but they retired to a horse stud,' Roxy volunteered. 'We'll see how we're going for time, Steph, but we should drop in if we can.'

'Great,' said Stephanie, 'and she's a fabulous cook.'

They climbed higher and higher until they saw the sign to Vergina and took the exit.

The hotel Aigon was modest but clean and comfortable. Out of consideration for country propriety, they booked two double rooms and Donald decided Roxy and he would share so Stephanie and Brendon could share the other room. Brendon reacted uneasily being separated from Donald but it seemed it was taken out of his hands.

'Unless you two guys would rather share,' Stephanie asked tentatively.

'No, that'll be great if it's okay with you two,' Brendon said referring to the girls.

'Well, I think we know each other well enough by now, don't you think?' Roxy replied with a smile. 'And I don't think the proprietors would look too kindly on a noisy foursome bouncing off the walls in the one room, do you?'

It was getting dark and as they were tired from the trip and with not much in the way of nightlife, they decided to eat locally and rise early in the morning for their visit to the nearby archaeological sites. Dinner was delicious local food and they retired reasonably early.

Donald quietly knocked on Brendon's door and when he answered he asked quietly, 'Do you have one of those Cialis tablets? I think I'm gonna need it.'

Brendon grinned and retired into the room where Stephanie was already naked, lying on the bed. Within a minute he returned to the door and handed Donald an orange sheaf of tablets. 'Don't take them all at once, 'Brendon warned, laughing. 'One should last you couple of days.'

'Right,' said Donald, pocketing the tablets, 'and you try and get some sleep if she'll let you,' he whispered as he turned to return to his room, 'Maybe it would've been less tiring if we'd hired a guide,' he said.

Brendon laughed. 'Remember, Alexander the Great had several wives he had to do his duty to – and one special boyfriend,' he added.

'God, how did he keep up his energy?' Donald replied with a groan, and disappeared down the hall.

When he arrived back in their room, Roxy was already in bed and it appeared as if she was already asleep. He stripped off and slipped into the double bed, trying not to disturb her but she roused.

'Sorry,' she said, 'it's been a big day.'

'That's okay,' he said, 'you go to sleep.' She closed her eyes and he lay on his side studying her profile. She really is quite beautiful, he thought. I wonder why she and Stephanie decided to become aid workers.

He drifted off to sleep but was awakened a few hours later by Roxy who had cuddled up to him and was gently stroking his body. Her hands wandered over his chest and nipples and slowly made her way down to his lower stomach and then on to his groin and lingered there. His penis automatically started to react and soon he was aroused to a full blown erection. He slipped his arm around her shoulders and pulled her close.

'I'm awake now,' she murmured in his ear and her lips and tongue explored his lobe.

'I can see that,' he said, enjoying the stimulation that spread over his entire body. He gently kissed her breasts and discovered her nipples had risen to the occasion. He then threw back the covers and turned on the bedside lamp which cast a soft pink glow over the room and her naked body.

Their love making was gentler with little of the spontaneous athletic activity of their previous session but it was none the less pleasurable. He caressed and kissed her, their tongues exploring each other's as their bodies melded in rapture. Roxy surrendered to his powerful thrusting, her eyes closed in ecstasy, sensations of ultimate pleasure overwhelming her entire body.

In Brendon and Stephanie's room, both slept soundly in the aftermath of spent passion; Brendon having done his duty.

Chapter 21

They stood at the entrance to the tombs, or tumulus as it was archeologically known, looking down the long grey stone pathway to the darkened opening. Archaeologists had been unearthing the concealed site since the 1860s suspecting they had discovered the remains of the ancient Agai location of the city of Valla. Eventually the entire area had been excavated including the theatre where it was believed King Philip the Second, father of Alexander the Great, had been murdered whilst attending the marriage of his daughter from another marriage, Cleopatra, to King Alexander of Epirus. Digging had continued with many interruptions until in the 1980s and 90s when archaeologists claimed they had discovered the tombs of the ancient Macedonian Royal families. Of the seven tombs, most had remained miraculously unsacked, one of which indicated it was the tomb of Philip the Second.

Roxy and Stephanie had led the two men around the ruins and although it was difficult to tell the layout, the men were fascinated and walked side by side absorbing the site. Both Brendon and Donald appeared introspect as they wandered and occasionally they would glance at each other with a puzzled look. When they reached the site of the old theatre, Brendon suddenly stumbled, apparently shocked and disorientated at the vista he beheld. Donald quickly reached out and supported him asking if he was all right. Brendon nodded but made no comment as, after a long pause, they slowly continued on their way.

Now walking into the tombs and museum, Brendon was showing signs of being unsteady on his feet and sat on the low wall that edged the path. Donald sat beside him, obviously concerned. Brendon made a vague excuse that he'd hurt his ankle when he stumbled and assured Donald he would soon be all right and instructed the women to go ahead and they'd catch them up. Donald massaged his ankle and eventually they stood, testing his strength and Brendon nodded that he was okay. Almost with trepidation he entered the museum and tomb sites and suddenly stopped and whispered to Donald, conspiratorially, 'I have the strangest feeling,' he said massaging his temples, 'that I've been here before – like déjà vu. '

Donald hesitated, obviously confounded by Brendon's remark and looked at him questioningly but Brendon gave no further explanation.

With a new alertness they wandered around the exhibits until they came to a case that contained a magnificent golden larnax, a heavily inscribed and decorated box that had contained King Philip's bones and ashes and above that hung an even more magnificent golden grave crown in the shape of an oak leaf and acorn floral wreath. Brendon was transfixed by both items and suddenly Roxy's voice at their shoulder shocked him from his reverie.

'Did you see the magnificent wall frieze of the chariot race and wall paintings?' she asked.

'Yeah, they're great,' Brendon replied, recovering seemingly enthusiastically, 'and the cremation bed is fascinating,' but he was still mesmerised by the larnax and the grave crown.

'Are you all right, Brendon, you look a bit stunned,' she said.

'No, I'm fine,' he said, 'Do you mind if we go now? My ankle's playing up a bit.'

'Sure, 'Roxy said. 'We've covered most of the site and we've still got a lot to see today. I've got a first aid kit in the car so I'll strap your ankle up when we get back.'

'No, I'll be fine,' he said. 'I think I just need to rest it for a bit.'

'Now don't be a difficult patient,' she said, officiously. 'I'm a very strict nurse and I don't put up with any shit, no matter how big the patient,'

They returned to the car and as Roxy attended to the reluctant patient, Stephanie appeared.

'Guess what I found in the gift shop,' she said, handing a plastic bag to Brendon. 'I got you a present.' She withdrew a car sticker from the bag and handed it to him. On the sticker was printed one word: "Bucephalus". 'That was the name of Alexander's black horse and I thought it was most appropriate for the Jeep, don't you think?' she said laughingly.

'He tamed that horse from when it was wild and nobody else could ride it,' Roxy said, as she completed the strapping. 'He had it for over twenty years and rode it into every battle.'

'A very appropriate gift,' he said, a little distracted. Donald took it from him, walked around the back of the Jeep and stuck it on the back windscreen.

Their next stop was the Pella ruins a few kilometres away but they stopped for coffee and pastry at a beautiful hotel, the Kalaitzis, on a hilltop overlooking the stunning countryside. They sat on the outside stone paved terrace and stared out at the view as they ate and drank their coffee.

'You know,' Brendon said, 'I could really get to like this part of the country; it is absolutely beautiful. It really resonates with me.'

'Does it?' Roxy replied. 'With all the bloodshed over the millennia, I always feel a sense of gloom over it.'

'What?' Donald said, amazed. 'How can you say that? I love it too.'

'I suppose I'm just used to it,' she replied, 'but there's always been a history of violence around here. The surrounding tribes were always at it and then came the Persians and then of course, Philip the Second and his nutty son and the Thracians and a stack of Slavic tribes and the Romans and the area copped it again in the World Wars. That's got to have an effect on the psyche of the people and the area,' she pronounced. 'I always seem to sense it. Too much reading, I suppose: overactive imagination.'

'But that's been the history of Europe and Asia through the ages,' Brendon said, in defence. 'Where would the world be without conquest? It brings in new ideas and development. Growth.'

'Tell that to the locals who had to go through it,' she replied cynically. 'Wait till you see the immediate results of conquest and power when we get to the refugee camps. It's always the ordinary people who suffer.'

'I rather liked that golden grave crown back at Vergina,' Stephanie broke in attempting to defuse what she sensed was turning into a strong disagreement. 'It'd go beautifully with my long white dress at the Embassy balls.'

'Bit heavy to wear, dear, and it wouldn't go with your runners,' Roxy replied with a laugh. 'Okay,' she said, rising, 'let's get on to Pella. That's where Alexander was born, educated and grew up in the lap of luxury. One of his teachers was Aristotle, did you know? Aristotle presented him with a copy of the Illiad which he carried around with him all the time. So he must've been a romantic as well.

'He was a big worshipper of the God Zeus, too,' she informed them,' he represented the God of justice and mercy and protector of the weak, would you believe?' she said, disdainfully. 'Alexander sure didn't show much mercy and he certainly didn't protect the weak; he slaughtered them. Zeus's weapon was a thunderbolt, Alexander's was his army and dick which he mainly used on Hephaestion.'

'Hep who? Donald asked.

'Hephaestion,' Brendon said. 'Alexander's supposed lifetime lover. You're a fund of information,' Brendon continued a little jealously to Roxy, 'but Alexander's remained a legend.'

'So have Hitler and Attila the Hun,' Roxy replied, snidely. 'I know my Greek history,' she said, 'I always hated it but it somehow stuck. By the way, it's wise never to call a Macedonian "Greek", they're a bit touchy about it. The southern Greeks refer to the Macedonians as primitive Slavs.'

Pella was magnificent in its destruction. It had been a huge capital city that had been virtually wiped out by earthquakes and rebuilt over the ruins. Doric columns rose to the heavens, the remains of well constructed houses, mosaic floors and porticos and in the centre, a pebbled mosaic atrium which acted as the ancient markets.

Alexander and his boyhood friend Hephaestion, had both been born and educated here the guide told them and the archaeologists thought they had discovered the site of where the two young men had been educated by Aristotle and others at Meiza. It was still being excavated and it was yet to be confirmed.

In contrast to the earlier site in Vergina, Donald and Brendon, whose ankle seemed to have miraculously recovered, practically ran around the site exploring the ruins. Roxy and Stephanie watched them in amused fascination as they idly wandered around.

'You don't think they could possibly be gay, do you, Roxy?' Stephanie asked dubiously, as her eyes followed the two men frolicking amongst the ruins.

'Not from recent experience,' Roxy replied, with a lecherous smile, 'but you never know in this day and age. Gay guys always seem to be the best looking and these two are gorgeous! If they are they certainly cover it well.'

Eventually the two men returned to the women and they made their way back to the car and climbed in, exhausted. But this time Donald and Brendon automatically climbed into the back seat together and Stephanie joined Roxy in the front passenger seat and cast a suspicious glance at Roxy and raised one eyebrow in question. Knowing exactly what was on Stephanie's mind, Roxy shrugged.

'Well, you two boys seem reinvigorated,' she said. 'Must be the air – or the company.'

'Definitely the company,' Donald laughed back. 'Where are we off to now?'

'Thessaloniki, on the coast,' Roxy replied. 'It's only about eighty kilometres away. If we decide to stay overnight we'll have to get away first thing in the morning. There's still a lot to see before Istanbul.'

They booked into the luxurious Daois Hotel that overlooked the Aegean Sea and the rooms and the views were superb. At the reception as Brendon was registering for the usual two double rooms, Roxy whispered to him, 'Would you mind if Steph and I shared tonight? We have a few things to talk over and we're both pretty exhausted. You boys wouldn't mind sharing, would you?'

Brendon glanced at Donald, who could hardly control his expectations at this prospect, and nodded, casually. 'No, that'd be just fine. He doesn't smell as good as you but I guess we'll cope.'

They agreed to meet for dinner in the dining room and both couples entered their rooms. Donald and Brendon threw their overnight bags on the luggage bench and turned to face each other.

'I think they might've guessed,' said Brendon.

'Who cares,' replied Donald.

'Come here, Patrocius,' Brendon said, holding out his arms.

'Who?' Donald asked.

'Patrocius, that was Alexander's nickname for Hephaestion.'

'Jesus,' said Donald, 'now he thinks he's fucking Alexander the Great! Make up your mind.'

Chapter 22

They met for dinner and chatted amicably, reviewing their experiences of the trip so far and their plans for the next day but there was definitely a difference in their relationship; not hostile but, more restrained. Brendon and Donald were relaxed and chatted, laughed and reminisced constantly. The girls joined in and the company was very compatible. After dinner they had coffee and liqueurs on the balcony overlooking the northern end of the Thermaic Gulf with Mount Olympus in the far distance.

Brendon suggested an after dinner stroll around the enormous Aristotelous Square but the girls declined, saying they were ready for bed and excused themselves. Brendon and Donald decided they should take a look at the famous square before they left this beautiful city and wandered off. Alone together, they explored the openness of the square with the surrounding beautiful Government buildings, hotels and the roadside *tavernas* that ringed the square. A comfortable contentment settled over them. They discovered a statue of Aristotle standing in the square and stopped to examine it.

'This used to be called Alexander Square originally,' Brendon told Donald, 'but apparently the city was nearly destroyed in a fire 1917 and almost the entire city had to be rebuilt. I read in my book that there used to be a statue of Alexander here somewhere but I can't see it. So obviously Alexander was pretty famous here as well.' He paused thoughtfully, studying the statue. 'I don't know why Roxy is so against him. His exploits have lasted through history. I wonder if it was because he had a male lover. Some women are funny that way. He did have three or four wives and one son to Rhoxana so he must've been home sometimes.

'What happened to the kid?' Donald asked.

'Killed with his mother after Alexander died. She knew it was on the cards so she took the boy back to Macedonia hoping for protection from Alexander's mum but the opposition generals caught up with them. Mind you, she'd already killed off Alexander's other wives to make sure her son would be the only successor and neither of them were already pregnant with his child. You couldn't be too careful in those days.'

'Nice lady, single-minded,' Donald quipped. 'Gawd, Alexander was a bit of a goer in the sex department, wasn't he? And you reckon I'm insatiable.'

After a leisurely nightcap at one of the roadside bars, watching the predominantly young crowds happily enjoying the area and atmosphere, they decided to return to their hotel.

There was no sign of Roxy and Stephanie and Brendon went to the reception and paid their bill, saying they would be leaving early in the morning and asking if they would they give him an early morning call to wake them.

Back in their room they undressed and wandered out onto the balcony to watch the moon shining on the water like a silver pathway to heaven.

'I'm so glad we came on this trip together,' Brendon murmured. 'I might not have discovered I was a famous Renaissance artist as I had hoped but just spending the time with you has been more than enough.'

Donald stood behind him and wrapped his arms around his waist. 'Likewise,' he whispered in Brendon's ear. 'I always pictured myself getting married and having six kids and a mother-in-law from hell and following the natural order of things. Life throws up some funny curve balls, doesn't it?'

'You just used a forbidden label, my friend, "natural",' Brendon responded with a smile. 'Nothing seems unnatural when I'm with you. In fact it's the most natural feeling in the world.'

'Well,' Donald said turning him around to face him, 'let's go to bed and be au-naturale together, eh?'

They made love with the same excitement and passion they had experienced since their first encounter in Brendon's studio.

Little did they know, in the next room, Roxy and Stephanie were also locked together in a sexual union of the same intensity. They too had discovered the joys of same sex coupling years before, driven by their enforced closeness, trust and intimacy in the implicit dangers they faced in strange foreign countries. They too considered themselves bi-sexual and enjoyed the sexual company of both men and each other but were never tempted by other women which protected them from ridiculous jealousies and unjustified loyalties and freed them from social constraint, giving them a feeling of sharing themselves equally if the occasion arose for personal and mutual satisfaction. They also showed no preference seeing their needs as an appetite to be satisfied with a person they loved or were deeply attracted to and saw no reason to be overt in their behaviour and risk defamation of their characters by some who still held current social inhibitions on acceptable behaviour that still silently persisted. That is why they had so enjoyed the sexual foursome they shared with Brendon and Donald; as Donald had said, 'the best of both worlds'.

Chapter 23

The next morning they arrived in the foyer, bright and cheery and ready for the day's adventures. Donald automatically sat in the front passenger seat and Brendon and Stephanie shared the back seats. There was no discussion; it just happened that way.

'Olalalala!' Roxy whooped, copying the war cry of the ancient Macedonians. She was forced to explain her outcry to the men who delightedly took up the call immediately as they sped through the early dawn traffic to the sounds of accompanying car horns.

They drove east between the coast and over the mountainous, verdant countryside and a new exhilaration filled them. They took a side exit to a little sea port town called Kavala, an ancient tobacco port which had now become quite ritzy, and passed the local sites of the fortified castle the Acropolis, Mosques, churches and converted store houses and marvelled at the preponderance of red roofs. Roxy turned and headed towards the mountains without stopping for further sightseeing. Soon they came to a private turnoff which Roxy took and after a couple of miles, and found themselves in a beautiful verdant green valley with a stream passing through on its way to the Aegean. She pulled into the entrance of a beautiful treed garden property, beeping the horn, and pulled up. Their friends, Alexius and Aikaterine hurried from the old stone building to greet them.

'This used to be a tobacco plantation,' Roxy said as she engaged the handbrake, 'but now Alexius runs horses. If you're nice to him he might let you have a ride while we chat with Aikaterine. They're Greek so for God's sake don't refer to them as Macedonians.'

Alexius and his wife were a lovely, elderly Greek couple whose children had moved to Melbourne, which wasn't unusual in Greece, and welcomed them profusely. They had befriended Roxy and Stephanie in Istanbul when the girls had first been posted there with *Sans Frontières*. Alexius was a doctor and his wife a nurse, whom he called Katherine, and they had taken the girls under their wing and shown them the ropes of surviving in the hell house refugee camps.

They sat on the front terrace and Aikaterine served them home made Turkish bread, a variety of cheeses, olives, dips and wine as they chatted and caught up on the latest gossip from the front line which didn't seem to be getting any better. To escape the endless chatter, Alexius then invited Brendon and Donald down to the stables where they examined his fine stable of horses.

With Donald's childhood experience of horses he was obviously knowledgeable about their excellent condition and was particularly interested in a skittish, fine dark brown, almost black, stallion by the name of Brutus. To Alexius' surprise, Donald had an almost immediate rapport with the stallion, stroking and whispering to him until Brutus settled down and accepted him.

Alexius asked if they'd like a ride and they eagerly accepted. The young stable hand saddled up Brutus and a mare called Roxana which he claimed he'd named after Roxy but, of course, it was also the name of Alexander the Great's first wife and mother of his only child, Alexander the fourth. She had been an Afghani and the sixteen-year-old daughter of a minor baron Alexander had defeated, which one wouldn't imagine would encourage a happy marriage but Alexander had married her to help reinforce his power over the Persians but she was also said to be the most beautiful woman in Afghanistan.

Donald and Brendon rode their mounts around the property robustly and in great excitement and Brendon was amazed at Donald's dexterity when matched against his own merely competent skill. Brendon had only ridden socially and Donald laughed at his lack of expertise as he wheeled, jumped and turned at speed always in full control of his mount. They both felt the heart racing thrill of the ride with the wind blowing in their faces and feeling the power of their horses beneath them as they trotted and galloped. They eventually pulled up in front of the terrace and the women dutifully clapped. Excited and stimulated by their ride, Brendon and Donald made their way back to the stables.

'Are you girls serious about these two young men?' Aikaterine asked.

Roxy and Stephanie laughed. 'No, they're just a couple of Aussie friends we met up with in Florence,' Stephanie replied.

'That is good,' Aikaterine answered, nodding her head wisely. 'They are far too pretty to marry or be serious about. Always marry a plain man who will protect you and care for you and not be too distracted by other women. Look at my Alexius, plain as horse shit but always reliable. He was also good in love making too in the old days, he couldn't believe his luck. He thought every time might be his last.'

The girls laughed. 'Besides, we suspect they might be gay, they're very close,' Roxy said.

'Ah, that is not good,' Aikaterine said disapprovingly. 'There will be no children.'

'It has been known to happen,' Roxy replied, dourly, 'but for us, children are right off the radar, thank you, there are too many in the world already. Look at the camps.'

The boys returned and they stood to go. 'We're sorry it was such a short visit,' Stephanie said, 'but we have to get on to Istanbul and the boys want to stop off at Gallipoli on the way.'

'Ah, more unnecessary suffering,' Aikaterine said, shaking her head. 'Men will never learn; they never have and they never will. War is in their blood which they have left all over the world while they deserted their widows and children and left nothing but lifelong hardship, sadness and pain.'

'That's why God made women like us,' Roxy smiled, 'to comfort, heal and look after them. And beat the guys up when they get out of hand,' she added, looking directly at Brendon and Donald. 'But they do come in handy sometimes.'

Gallipoli deeply troubled them as they drove through the sites of the battlegrounds and wandered through the cemeteries, past memorials that meant so little to the ones they immortalised but much to distant and dwindling family members who visited. Yet, according to latest reports it apparently seemed to be having more meaning to the ever growing numbers of young people who came as a pilgrimage to a past history they could never really understand. You had to be there to experience the carnage, the suffering and the senseless waste. But if the call came again they would probably respond as all young men seemed to do.

Roxy and Stephanie went their own way as Brendon and Donald, in contrast to their mood, had become particularly morose and detached as they witnessed the aftermath of the conflict and the thousands of graves of the young men, such as themselves, and younger, who rested there, never to have the chance to fulfil their potential as fathers, sons, brothers and men.

Brendon joined Donald sitting on a rock overlooking Anzac Cove, each sinking into a deep, dreamlike reverie picturing, or was it reliving, the fear and slaughter of the campaign. In their minds they heard the explosions of bombardment and machine-gun fire that ripped men's bodies apart, the screams of dying and mutilated men who had long ago stopped believing in the boyhood cause or patriotism and were only intent on surviving. They sat there silently watching the sea of the Dardanelles for a very long time both seemingly lost in a shared spiritual experience.

Suddenly Donald became aware of Brendon's soft voice breaking through the silence of his trancelike state. 'I'm sorry,' Brendon said, remorsefully, 'I couldn't save you.'

Without further explanation as to why Brendon had made that remark, Donald turned to look into Brendon's heartbreakingly sad face. Tears were gently streaming down his cheeks and dropping onto his shirt. Donald rose and embraced the man who had tried so desperately to save him so many times through the aeons of history but had forever failed and Donald's soul had risen into another dimension waiting for the opportunity to join him again.

That night, they stayed in the nearby luxurious Palazzo Del Corso hotel and there was no discussion as to who would share with whom. There would be no sex that night but Brendon and Donald slept in each other's loving, protective embrace.

Chapter 24

Istanbul immediately lifted their spirits. Roxy drove them through the horrendous traffic of the city to their apartment overlooking the bustling, paved, Taksim Square with its famous red trams, packed to overflowing with passengers hanging from the sides. Fascinating shops and smells of every description lined the square and from the balcony of their two bedroom apartment they were mesmerised by the constant activity and couldn't wait to join the throng.

For two days Brendon and Donald explored the fabulous city taking in the cobbled streets and the narrow lanes and the treasures of centuries; the Grand Bazaar, with its jostling locals and tourists hunting for the exotic and utilitarian, the magnificent Topkapi Palace with its crown jewels and a circumcision room, which neither really needed, the Beautiful Blue and Suleyanive mosques overlooking the Bosphorus by night and of course the architecturally brilliant Yeni Camii and the myriad other tourist sites of the city. Of course they toured the magnificent Istanbul Archaeological museum for the Alexander the Great collection and were amazed at the lustrous white marble sarcophagus, the sides of which were adorned with beautiful reliefs of Alexander, spear upraised over his right shoulder, ready for battle on his faithful horse, Bucephalus, who was depicted rearing up over a fallen Persian horseman, and on the other side another of Alexander on a hunt. This was originally thought to be where Alexander's remains had been deposited only to find out that it actually belonged to a gardener named, Abdalonymus, whom Alexander had appointed as local leader in Sidon. Apparently the gardener, in death as he had in life wanted to continue to honour his overlord and had his sarcophagus decorated in that manner to do so. Alexander's final resting place remains unknown but it is suspected he was returned to Macedon.

Although unspoken, Roxy and Stephanie had quite accepted the boy's relationship though occasionally the four would again revisit the sexual exploits of Florence for the sheer beauty and lustful experience. The girls contacted their headquarters and were soon called upon to make trips to southern Turkey to give assistance in the worsening refugee situation on the Syrian border. On their return they would regale the boys with shocking tales of their experiences and gradually the boys became fascinated with the details of their excursions.

One morning, over breakfast, Donald finally broached the subject he and Brendon had been discussing in private. 'Would there be any chance of Brendon and I taking a look at the camps?'

Roxy and Stephanie shared a puzzled look. 'Are you sure?' Roxy asked. 'They're pretty terrible.'

'Well,' Brendon said, 'I've been thinking about what you said back in Florence; about a painting exhibition based on the refugees. It might be a good idea; a series of portraits and maybe a landscape or two. It could bring a bit of publicity to the cause and maybe help Sans Frontiers in their charity work. Sometimes paintings can bring a more sympathetic reaction than the real life news footage plastered over the newspapers and ten second grabs on Television. The public have become desensitised to suffering and war.'

The girls shared a questioning look. 'Tell you what, 'Roxy said, 'I'll have a word with my superiors and see if they'd agree to supporting it. You're right, it could be a good thing.'

'We'd drive down of our own accord,' Donald said, 'because we'd like to see a bit more of the country before we have to head back home.'

'It could be a bit dangerous,' Stephanie warned. 'The Turkish security do their best but there always seems to be rebel groups suddenly turning up and causing trouble. The security services can't be everywhere at once.'

'I'm pretty sure we can look after ourselves,' Donald answered, 'and besides it'll only be for a couple of days and Brendon can take a lot of photos to work from and get a feel of the place. I don't think he actually wants to sit subjects down to pose for him while he paints them. And certainly not naked like his last exhibition, I hope,' he added.

Brendon assured him that he could actually paint portraits of people with their clothes on and agreed with him but they were interrupted by the girls receiving a call from Sans Frontier telling them they were to deliver a consignment of much needed drugs to the Syrian border camps near Kilis and that there was word of another border infringement nearby they were to check out. They would be choppered down and guarded by Turkish Security forces while they were there.

'We'll take off as soon as we can and meet up with you in Kilis,' Brendon said. 'Will that be all right?'

The girls shared a worried look and told them to wait until they received confirmation from their bosses. The boys agreed and began their own preparations for their trip. They decided they'd start anyway as they were quite looking forward to seeing more of the Turkish countryside and if they were refused there was still plenty to see and they'd make their way back to Istanbul before they were due to leave for Australia. Within a couple of hours the boys were on the road heading south west over the Bosphorus Bridge and into Asia Minor towards the ruins of Troy. Little did they realise they were roughly following in Alexander's footsteps.

They arrived at the seaside resort of Canakkale about half an hour from the ruins of Troy and were surprised at the size and beauty of the town, perched on the shores of the Dardanelles. They decided to stop for coffee and to take a look around the place and snap some photographs. On the foreshore by a large square they were awestruck by a huge representation of the wooden Trojan horse the Greeks had used to trick the Trojans in the battle for Troy. Brendon was particularly impressed with the beautiful statue of a brilliant white flying Unicorn which stood near the ferry terminal. They wandered around captivated by the place and the number of tourists ogling the sites. Eventually they came across a delightful *taverna* on the waterside and stopped to rest and recuperate with coffee and a snack. They decided the place was definitely worth exploring further with maybe a night stopover and Donald was particularly interested in visiting the ancient Kalitbahir fortress that still stood guard over the town. But as they finished their snack and were preparing to leave Brendon's mobile phone rang.

The call was from Roxy who told him she had been able to get permission for them to visit but it could only be for a few hours as the authorities weren't encouraging the press or sightseers owing to the appalling conditions existing in the camps. Brendon thanked her profusely and told her where they were and that they would leave immediately for `Kilis, on the Syrian border. They arranged to meet and Brendon informed her he'd ring as soon as they arrived and they would get there as fast as they could.

'Well,' he said, switching off his phone and turning to Donald, 'I'm afraid our tour of Troy is going to have to wait until we come back. We'll whip down to Kilis, meet up with the girls, take a few photos and make our way back up here, okay?'

'Fine with me,' replied Donald as they stood and hurried towards the car.

Roxy met them in Kilis at the prearranged spot and they transferred into the Sans Frontier ambulance she was driving, leaving the Jeep with Stephanie who was on duty at a small, crowded, canvas tent medical centre nearby. The boys were astounded at the number of refugees roaming the streets as if lost, mostly women and children and old men who had fled from their homes in Syria. Most of the women, though dressed in Western style, were Muslim and still wore the hijab or scarves to cover their heads.

Roxy then drove them as close as possible to the border crossing where thousands of refugees were waiting to pass into Turkey and Roxy brought the ambulance to a stop. Brendon excitedly grabbed his camera and jumped out, immediately lining up subjects for photographs. 'They're mostly housed in tents or containers all paid for by the Turkish Red Crescent relief organisation,' Roxy said to Donald who was peering around, fascinated by the unruly throng of people. 'It will be hell for them in winter,' she said, 'and a lot of the younger men cross back and forth into Syria to join the rebels fighting the Government forces or work at their jobs and leave their women and children here in relative safety. Some also go back and escort other relatives or friends to the border too; it's never ending.'

Donald indicated a long queue of refugees lining up for water and pointed them out to Brendon who was already busy taking photos. The congestion of humanity was horrendous and clamouring noise and desperation was in the air.

'This camp is relatively well organised for its size,' she said. 'Some enterprising souls have even set up cafés and barbershops and the women sew, do the laundry, cook and look after the thousands of children. The locals were quite welcoming in the beginning but I think it's wearing a bit thin now. There's been no available accommodation since just after first influx of refugees arrived so the Government set up the camps; not the Hilton, maybe, but safer than their homes back in Syria.'

She was interrupted by her mobile phone ringing and answered. 'What?' she said, 'where?' She waited while the person on the other end explained the situation. 'Well, we can drive up and take a look,' she said,' and I'll report back to you.' She switched off the phone and turned to Donald. 'Just had word of another illegal crossing further west from here and I've been asked to go in and evaluate the situation.

We'll check if anyone needs medical attention and notify headquarters.'

Donald called to Brendon to get back in the ambulance as they had to go and Brendon threw himself back in the front seat, squeezing Donald over closer to Roxy. She slowly reversed the vehicle, with siren bellowing, careful to avoid any pedestrians or small children until she found a spot where she could safely turn, then, relative to safety, she moved the car forward as fast as possible again with the siren bellowing. When she had a clear run she hit the accelerator and headed out of town where the traffic was lighter and sped west.

Chapter 25

They approached the Syrian border which was really nothing more than a barbed wire fence much further up and noticed a small group of refugees, men, women and children, some being carried in their mother's arms, crossing into Turkey.

'They get impatient with waiting in the long queues and sometimes make their way further west to cross. The Turkish security tries to dissuade them so they can remain in control but the problem is so vast it's difficult to cover the entire border. They have to check there aren't any weapons being smuggled over,' she said. 'I'll take the co-ordinates,' she continued, as she pulled out her smart phone, 'and phone them back.'

She pulled up and they got out of the car for a better idea of the situation and at that moment they heard the whine of fighter plane overhead. A rocket suddenly exploded close to the fleeing refugees on the Syrian side and many refugees were caught in the explosion.

'Fucking Syrian air force,' Roxy screamed looking up at the already climbing fighter plane and they all dived for cover under the Jeep for protection from the shrapnel and flying debris from the rocket. They buried their faces in the ground waiting for another attack while the surviving refugees screamed and scattered, trying to find cover. After that single attack the plane turned and flew back in the direction it had come from and the three observers scrambled from cover and ran to see if they could help the wounded and survivors. There were many victims lying on the ground, some badly wounded with missing limbs and others bleeding and crying out in pain and they attempted to assist them the best way they could. As they did they heard more planes approaching and they readied themselves for another attack but looking up, Roxy yelled, 'It's all right, they're Turkish!' The Turkish fighters set off to intercept the Syrian interloper.

But as they bent over the wounded another danger faced them as they heard machine-gun fire from a distance whipping around them. They hit the ground and looked in the direction of this new assault. Six Syrian soldiers were running toward them with guns at the ready and screaming for them to lie down. Ignoring their orders, Roxy ran for the ambulance to get a first aid kit. The boys went to follow but there was a burst of machine gun fire and a bullet grazed Brendon's head, the impact knocking him to the ground. Donald yelled Brendon's name in horror and dropped down next to him. 'You bastards!' he yelled trying to stem the trickle of blood from Brendon's head. 'We're Australians from the *Sans Frontières* medical unit, you fucking mongrels, and we're on Turkish ground!'

The apparent leader, a monstrously big man with a black beard, dressed in military fatigues, ordered his men to stop firing and approached Donald with Brendon lying next to him on the ground, conscious but obviously dizzy from his wound.

'Where's Adad?' the monster yelled in English, realising they weren't Arabic.

'Adad?' Donald yelled back. 'Who the fuck is Adad?'

'Adad Omar,' the leader yelled back. 'The traitor from the People's Government, the minister for cowardice. The pig is trying to escape into Turkey to save his own skin. But we will kill him before he does that.'

'I told you we're from *Sans Frontières* – the Turkish Red Crescent and we've got nothing to do with your fucking war!' Donald tried hard to restrain the anger that was exploding in him like a time bomb. 'Look what you've done to these innocent people!' he yelled.

The leader ignored him and gave instructions to his men in Arabic and they all spread out searching the dead and wounded for their quarry but apparently the quarry wasn't among the victims of the attack. The huge swarthy leader gave an order and his men began dragging the survivors back over the border.

Taking advantage of the momentary distraction, Donald, knowing Roxy had gone back to the ambulance, called out, 'Roxy, for Christ's sake go! Get help!' Roxy's head suddenly appeared from behind the ambulance and he gestured frantically. She hesitated and he gestured again urgently, pointing back towards the camp. She sprang into action and threw herself into the driver's seat, switched on the ignition and roared off. The soldiers, caught unawares, fired after her but she had been too fast. Donald sank down over his friend.

The angry leader, having been thwarted, walked over to Donald and Brendon lying on the ground and aimed a vicious kick at Donald's head. Donald automatically grabbed the boot and twisted, throwing the leader off balance. The leader hit the ground with a loud thump and Donald immediately prepared himself to launch an attack but the click of guns cocking stopped him in his tracks and he froze. Seemingly unperturbed, the leader rose from the ground and stood looking down on Donald with menace in his cold, black eyes. Donald immediately went into defence mode.

Suddenly the leader turned away and growled in Arabic to his men and then switched to English as he turned to Donald. 'It is getting dark and your *friend* will no doubt be on her way to inform the security forces so we will go.' He looked at Donald and Brendon and the few remaining survivors. 'And you and your friends will come with us as a shield if the security force catch up with us. Come!'

'Where are you taking us?' Donald demanded.

'To our secret camp. Get your friend on his feet or I will leave him here, dead with the others.' He turned to his men and issued another order in Arabic.

The remaining terrorists calmly walked up to every man lying on the ground and put a bullet in their heads. Donald was horrified.

'I'm okay,' Brendon suddenly murmured to Donald. 'It just knocked me about a bit but I'll recover,' he said getting to his feet groggily. Donald supported him around the shoulders as they and the four other survivors were forced to follow their captor and his five accomplices at the point of an AK47.

They tramped for what seemed like hours until they came to a small valley. Staggering down the slope they came to the mouth of a cave hidden by boulders and shrubbery and were forced inside, the leader leaving a couple of guards outside. They were ordered to sit. Donald helped Brendon to lie on the floor while he sat on a rock nearby. The soldiers made a small fire which gave a little light and warmth in the otherwise darkened cave.

'Now what?' Donald asked the leader who he now discovered was named Sargon.

Sargon smiled, displaying yellowing teeth. 'We eat, we wait and if they discover us, we negotiate,' he said. 'And if they don't find us,' he added, 'you will be shot and left here, probably never to be found.'

'Have you got a dressing I can put on my friend's head?' Donald asked, trying to distract the conversation away from their likely execution.

Sargon spoke to one of the soldiers who opened his pack, withdrew a field dressing and threw it to Donald who tore it open and tended Brendon's small head wound.

'I think we've got ourselves into some deep shit here,' Brendon muttered as Donald applied the dressing.

'Momentarily, maybe,' Donald replied quietly, 'but if I know Roxy she'll be organising a rescue and we just have to survive until they find us.'

A pretty young girl named Ishtar, who looked to be no more than fifteen and on the verge of womanhood, sat close beside Donald for protection and watched him with fear written on her lovely face. The other women refugees sat huddled together on the opposite side of the cave. He smiled kindly at Ishtar trying to reassure her and whispered instructions in her ear.

One of the soldiers pulled a food pack from his backpack, laid out a dirty ground sheet and started preparing a meal. Sargon settled back and lit a joint, inhaling the pungent smoke deep into his lungs.

They ate only morsels of food as there was not enough to go around and many of the women refused or were unable to eat out of fear. The night wore on and Sargon continued to smoke and watch the captives, speculatively. The other soldiers lit up joints and began to relax. Donald and Brendon shared a conspiratorial look.

'I don't think these are regulars,' Brendon whispered to Donald. 'I think they're a pack of loners, common opportunists. And I think they're after ransom.'

Donald shrugged. 'Doesn't make a lot of difference,' he replied. 'We're still swimming upstream in shit.'

'Keep your eyes open, they're getting higher by the minute. They might get careless.'

'Shut up!' Sargon snapped, as he scratched his balls. But obviously it wasn't itchy balls that were bothering him from the look on his face as he studied Ishtar. Donald knew that look and prepared for action: action that could get them all killed.

Sargon rose to his feet and stood looking down at Ishtar with hungry eyes and Donald and Brendon tensed, ready to protect the young terrified girl. Sargon unzipped his trousers and they fell to the ground revealing the longest, thickest, ugliest penis they had ever seen short of a rutting stallion, standing erect as a missile ready for launch.

'Lay off, Sargon,' Brendon growled warningly. 'She's only a kid and probably a virgin. Put your dick away and keep your filthy hands off her.'

'I said shut up!' Sargon roared. He bent and grabbed his pistol from its holster and pistol whipped

Brendon on his head, reopening his wound and sending him unconscious to the floor. Already tensed, Donald jumped to his feet and threw himself at Sargon, punching him heavily on the jaw.

The sudden commotion awoke the refugees who started screaming and huddling closer together for protection. The two outside guards came running into the cave and dropped their guns to help subdue Donald who fought ferociously using every dirty trick he could to evade them: kicking, punching, gouging, lashing out with anything at hand, his fury unrestrained. 'Run, Ishtar, run!' he yelled over the screaming women.

Ishtar grabbed the opportunity and scuttled through the mouth of the cave into the black night. This encouraged the other women who also took advantage of the mayhem erupting around them and ran for their lives after Ishtar.

But the odds were against Donald and eventually he was overcome by the sheer weight of numbers. Two of the soldiers restrained him, holding him firmly by his shoulders and forced him to stand in front of their still erect leader. Sargon slapped him viciously across the face and continued to smile, his eyes dilated from cannabis.

'Aw, you took away my virgin fuck,' he said ruefully, in his heavily accented English. 'Now what will I do?'

'You could go fuck yourself,' Donald suggested.

Suddenly Sargon grabbed the neck of his shirt and ripped it the entire length.

'Ah, no, I think I have a better idea,' he said, the evil smile returning to his face.

He barked out an order to the men holding Donald and they immediately laughed and tore the rest of his clothes off him, leaving him vulnerable and naked, apart from his socks and runners. They then manhandled him over to the rock he had been sitting on and forced him to lie face down on it, their strong arms preventing his struggles.

Sargon stood at his feet and suddenly kicked Donald's legs apart.

'Nice young, firm body, 'Sargon said appraising him.

Donald knew exactly what was about to happen and although he struggled hopelessly his heartbeat went crazy and his stomach began to churn, he was helpless, hopelessly pinned down by Sargon's men. The other men stood around laughing and obviously egging Sargon on and jokingly indicating which one would go next as they laid aside their weapons and also dropped their trousers in preparation for a pack gang rape.

Donald's mind suddenly became frighteningly clear as he knew exactly what was about to happen to him. He tried to relax his muscles knowing tense muscles would only make it worse but when it happened the shock was so great, a stifled roar of pain escaped his throat as Sargon suddenly launched his deadly weapon hard into Donald's anus. The other men howled in laughter at the vicious attack. Donald's body shuddered and twitched in agony. The pain was excruciating as he felt the skin around his anus tear and the feeling of Sargon's massive penis, viciously thrusting into him like a jackhammer, seemed to even invade his chest and stomach like a rod of burning steel but he attempted to stifle any sound that would give his attackers any further satisfaction. His time would come for revenge, of that he was certain.

The sound of the laughing and Donald's stifled scream cut through Brendon's consciousness and his eyes flew open to behold the brutal scene before him, made worse by the flickering fire that conjured up a scene from Dante's 'Inferno'. In the periphery of his vision he became aware of one of the AK47s that one of the soldiers had dropped trying to subdue Donald.

With every ounce of his remaining strength he shot out his arm and grabbed the gun, flicked off the safety catch, aimed and coolly pressed the trigger.

The initial burst of gunfire caught Sargon in the chest, which seemed to explode as the bullets tore the life from him and blood shot in the air in crimson spurts. The long burst continued and moved on catching the surprised attackers and onlookers unprepared for their deaths as the bullets mercilessly continued to rip their bodies apart and skin, blood, bones and brains flew through the air, tiny projectiles of worthless lives that once were. After only a few seconds, the stuttering gunfire stopped and a sudden silence, broken only by Donald's pitiful stifled groans, reigned in the cave.

Brendon threw the gun aside and rushed to his friend. He gently helped him to his feet and held him close feeling the torture and ignominy his friend had been forced to sustain. Donald hugged him tightly and Brendon whispered, 'Come and lie down.'

'If it's all the same to you,' Donald winced as he replied, 'I think I might just stand until I can visit the nearest proctologist who has morphine and a needle and thread. My arse is in shreds.'

Brendon was forced to laugh in spite of himself. 'Now we've got to work out where the hell we are and how to get out of here,' he said supporting Donald as he stood.

'If you look in my right sock and sneaker, you'll find your mobile tucked there,' Donald uttered. 'I hid it down there when they did that paltry search back at the border. You've got overseas roaming; you should be able to get onto Roxy. They can pick up the signal.'

Brendon hugged him again and bent to look in his sock and runner. The mobile was still tucked exactly where Donald had described it and Brendon was relieved.

'I would've got it myself but it hurts to bend,' Donald explained. 'There goes our sex life for a while.'

Brendon stood up just in time for the bullet to smash into his head. One of the soldiers had used his dying breath and last vestige of strength to clumsily lift his AK47 and fire off a single round before dropping back on the ground. The shot was meant for Donald.

Donald bellowed in horror as his lover dropped to the ground.

Chapter 26

A *Sans Frontières* chopper arrived very soon afterwards. Donald, ignoring his own pain had scrambled for the mobile phone and punched in Roxy's number. After an endless wait, she finally answered and Donald quickly gave her the situation. She was appalled and rang off as soon as she had established the co-ordinates of their location. He then searched the backpacks of the dead men for first aid kits and managed to stop Brendon's bleeding. It was only then Donald noticed the wounded and now semi-conscious and groaning militiaman who had shot Brendon and in his pain and anger, he snatched up the AK47 and shot the man in the head. Then he coolly went around and shot the others again including Sargon, in revenge for the pain and humiliation they had caused him. He felt nothing as the bullets ripped through their bodies.

It seemed to take forever for the chopper to arrive and when he heard the motors, Donald stumbled out of the cave and waved frantically to signal them. Naturally Roxy and Stephanie were with the doctors and other medical staff and they worked quickly and efficiently. Amazingly Brendon was still alive and they stretchered him out to the chopper for evacuation to the nearest hospital. Donald insisted on sitting and watching over his friend, willing him to live. He had to be physically restrained and pulled away from Brendon so the medics could do their work.

Donald was examined and the damage Sargon had inflicted on him was discovered and treated but after that he returned to watch over Brendon.

Brendon was patched up at the aid station and transferred back to Istanbul by helicopter. At the hospital Donald paced the corridor in discomfort while Brendon was in the operating theatre undergoing surgery. Still devastated, he sat by the hospital bed for the next four days and slept fitfully in a chair by the bed and his vigil continued.

Roxy and Stephanie came to visit when they could and organised food and coffee for him which he mostly ignored but they were unable to console him. Brendon remained in a coma that could last for days, months or forever and Donald was sick to his heart.

On the third day, Roxy stood in the doorway watching Donald's despair and noticed the tears running down his cheeks. She walked up behind him and gently laid her hand on his shoulder, 'You really do love him, don't you,' she said quietly

'More than my life itself,' he responded.

But Brendon was no longer of this world. His soul rose into another strange dimension and guides appeared to comfort him. Brendon couldn't actually see them but felt their loving presence and communicated with thoughts and pictures. He felt at incredible peace as they 'talked' and he indicated he wanted to know the answer to the questions that had been plaguing him. They told him he was only to see the incidents that affected him in his current incarnation because he hadn't fully achieved the spiritual development he had set himself and spiritual development was uppermost in development of the soul. Before he could move on he must achieve this or return again and again until he did. He seemed to be aware of flying through a maze of energy vibrating colours he could never imagine being able to mix on his palette and incredibly beautiful music which was unrecognisable yet somehow familiar.

He suddenly felt younger and immature as he looked at a 'screen' before him and saw a group of young boys sitting on silken cushions in front of a bearded, middle-aged man who was apparently teaching them. They were dressed in short, white tunics with white bandannas tied around their heads and wore sandals on their feet. The word *Meiza* flashed into his mind and he saw again the ruins they had recently visited and as he watched they grew in size and stature as if by a cinematic special effect until they were restored to their original magnificence.

He sensed the middle-aged man was incredibly wise and profound and that much of what he was teaching them was beyond his capacity to fully understand. The name Aristotle came to him and he suddenly seemed to zoom in to what seemed a cinematic close-up of a rugged, strong, handsome youth with short dark curly hair. But the 'camera' didn't stop and continued to zoom in until he became the youth. He turned to his left and saw sitting next to him a beautiful, blonde, curly-haired young man wearing a plaited gold band around his head, and who was arguing heatedly with their tutor. Although he felt reclusive and shy he also felt overwhelmed by this attractive young man sitting close beside him who gave the impression of being arrogant, proud, conceited and ambitious to others but to him he was a God. The beautiful blonde young man's face suddenly morphed into a face he knew so well. It was Donald! My God, Donald had been Alexander the Great! So – did that make Brendon, Alexander's lifelong lover, Hephaestion? The words of their tutor came into his mind. 'Fathered by the God Zeus: One soul, two bodies.'

Snippets of scenes flickered through his spiritual vision; he and the blonde young man running and wrestling, Donald, riding a magnificent black horse racing through the countryside, training for battle, throwing spears and shooting arrows at targets, laughing, fighting side by side as they perfected techniques of war. And then a scene that shocked him as he was attempting to paint a portrait of his reluctant naked boyhood friend who gloried in sculptures of himself but not paintings. Alexander suddenly stepped down from the podium he was standing on and stood looking at him in the same way that Donald had looked at him when he was painting his portrait for his exhibition. He felt again that same undeniable magnetism and they were soon entwined in an impassioned, naked embrace that lingered in his soul.

It was all laid out before him; Alexander's hated father, Philip the Second being murdered at his daughter's wedding celebrations in the theatre at Pella, after Philip had married Cleopatra of Eurydice, forcing Alexander and his conniving mother, Olympius, who suddenly morphed into Sylvia, the subject of his mourning widow painting, to flee to Epirus! He witnessed himself and Alexander in battle with the other Greeks states in the battle of Chaeronea and many others, their victories and Alexander becoming the undisputed king of a united Greece, their march at the head of a massive army to defeat the Thracians, their arrival in Troy with Alexander actually steering the leading vessel of the vast flotilla across the Dardanelles to the shore where he threw a spear into the sand to claim the territory. They had actually been welcomed by the Trojans and he and Alexander had laid a wreath of flowers each on the tomb of their heroes Achilles and his presumed lover, Patrocius, who had died there in the Battle of Troy, centuries before and been cremated together with their bones and ashes forever intertwined.

After the besieging of Giza and their subsequent victory, Brendon watched their army move on to Egypt where they were welcomed as saviours from the control of the marauding Persian Empire. Alexander was honoured by the populace and thought to be a god and Brendon was present when Alexander was glorified and sumptuously crowned as Pharaoh in the temple of Karnak in the city of Thebes.

The spoils had been enormous making the already fabulously rich Alexander even more wealthy and honoured but he grew even more arrogant, ambitious and determined to press on and become the undisputed Emperor of Persia or the world. Brendon was assigned to oversee the building of the beautiful city of Alexandria, another tribute to his lover.

Their subsequent invasion of Asia Minor and victories over the Persians, which Brendon beheld as a series of vicious, bloody battles where he and Alexander always lead their enormous armies into fierce battle, They planned strategy and fought ferociously side by side, mounted on their horses with spear, sword and shield, giving no quarter or pity. It finally ended with the defeat of King Darius the Third,' near the river Granceus, in Turkey. Brendon was surprised to discover that Darius' soul had moved on through many dimensions and incarnations, never shedding his need for power and conquest to evolve into the character of Jeremy, the sad, disillusioned old man Brendon had painted in the present day, wearing a wilting laurel wreath; an unplanned shade of past glories?

He experienced their torturous march over the desert into Iran to Babylon, the very heart of the Persian Empire and the magnificent crowning of Alexander as King of Persia, there. He also saw Babylon's disintegrate into the ruins of today which now overlook a palace built by Saddam Hussein, another deposed, conceited, power hungry leader or a product of reincarnation?

Then came other surprises: without Hephaestion, Alexander was called to quell a rebellion in Bactria, in Iraq. The Prince of Bactria, now miraculously morphed into the form of James, the mild subject of his Victorian family painting! Crystal, the lovely daughter, had unsurprisingly become a camp follower of Alexander's army bringing comfort to the fighting men. After the Prince's eventual surrender his beautiful but calculating daughter, Rhoxana offered herself to Alexander as his wife. He accepted mainly as a means to gain an even stronger hold over the Persian Empire. At a ripe and seductive beauty of sixteen years, Rhoxana, used a victory celebration of food and much wine to seduce the more than willing Alexander who was not averse to being seduced by, who men claimed, was the most beautiful woman in Persia. They were married in Babylon and Brendon witnessed the birth of

Alexander's son who would never succeed him as King.

Brendon's soul as Hephaestion, who by now was considered Alexander's official bodyguard, witnessed the wedding as Alexander's best man. But what staggered him was the beautiful bride. As the elaborate ceremony progressed, Brendon immediately recognised her as the now lustful Linda! He watched them consummate the marriage, with Linda, as Rhoxana, even then immoral, abandoned, licentious and demanding. But after Alexander had done his husbandly duty, he returned to the bed of his lover, Hephaestion, as they continued on their conquests.

At the head of an even larger army, Alexander forced the now weary and growingly discontented soldiers east towards the Indus and Ganges Rivers in the north of India, but the men rebelled at the appalling conditions and refused to go further. Alexander was forced to retreat back along the Indus to keep them committed to his aspirations. As Hephaestion, Brendon realised the men respected and trusted him unquestionably and he was able to convince them to follow their King to the end of the world if necessary in Alexander's ambitious quest to be king of the known world and replace Darius the Third as King of Kings.

But as they made their way back along the Indus they were attacked by a tribe of Malli warriors and, although Hephaestion fought desperately to protect his lover, Alexander was badly wounded and Hephaestion threw himself over his friend's body fighting ferociously to protect him. He succeeded and the warriors were fought off but Alexander's army, now led by Hephaestion, who Alexander had named as his second in command, headed north along the rugged Persian Gulf to Susa where Alexander rested and finally recovered and they returned to Babylon.

But the journey didn't end there. To reinforce his position, Alexander married Stateira, daughter of Darius who had been killed by his own men and who had then surrendered to Alexander. Alexander, showed great respect for his old enemy and his daughters and had Darius's body entombed at Persepolis. He ordered many of his generals to marry Persian women to consolidate his hold over the Empire. This brought much discontent within the ranks as they believed Alexander was becoming more conceited and ambitious, turning himself into a

Persian Emperor and denying his Macedonian heritage.

He chose Drypetis, sister of Stateira and Darius's other daughter, for Hephaestion to marry so that in the case of any issue by either man, they would be related as brothers-in-law and their descendents both of the prior King of Kings and the current one, would rule forever. But Brendon was staggered to recognise Alexander's new wife as Roxy and his own new Persian wife as Stephanie! The two sisters had returned together again in this present reincarnation to fulfil their destiny to husbands who had died young after only a few months of marriage.

And finally he saw Alexander's death in Babylon where he was planning his conquests of Rome and Carthage. He had been secretly poisoned and the man who was responsible was now none other than, Georgio, a captured slave and the evil seductive youth Brendon had painted in the Blue Mountain's bush holding out a pottery bowl. Did that bowl signify it contained the poison that had killed Alexander?

But by then he had witnessed his own death from fever eight months prior and had watched his distraught lover mourn and weep over his body for days before he was physically forced to relinquish his body and allow it to be cremated. He had been sad to leave his lifetime lover but overjoyed at witnessing the elaborate games and feasting that followed his funeral to celebrate and honour his life as Hephaestion. But Alexander continued to mourn inconsolably.

Brendon suddenly knew that his belief in reincarnation was justified and that many souls return in groups through various incarnations to sometimes interact with each other in even seemingly innocuous ways in their quest for soul experience and development; a king one life and a pauper the next if the soul didn't use its free will to advance, spiritually. How many times or in what context he and Donald had existed in the same time frames as lovers was not available to him. There had obviously been a link at Gallipoli where he had become so emotional but that link and others remained hidden; locked away in the Akashik records of eternity. But of one thing he was certain. He instinctively knew they were always to be soul mates, sometimes male, sometimes female, inextricably linked; almost like, one soul and two bodies.

Chapter 27

Donald had dropped off to sleep with his head on Brendon's chest. Suddenly he became aware of his head being stroked and thought for a moment it was Roxy or Stephanie come to wake him. But then he heard Brendon's deep, gentle voice. 'Hi mate,' he said softly, 'how ya doin'?'

Donald started in surprise and lifted his face to Brendon's. He was out of the coma at last! He grabbed Brendon's hand and kissed it. 'Fuck, you gave us a scare,' he said, smiling broadly. 'You're back.'

'How long have I been away?' Brendon asked, his strength slowly returning.

'Five very long days,' Donald replied. 'How are you feeling?'

'Well, obviously a lot better than I was,' Brendon smiled. 'I know this sounds trite but, what happened and where am I?'

Donald filled him in on their capture and the consequences and brought him up to date on Brendon's latest medical assessment. At first,

Brendon struggled to remember, his mind still occupied with the journey he had taken in the spirit life while his body and soul repaired itself but eventually he was able to get things into perspective and said, 'Hey, I'm hungry.'

Donald immediately pushed the call button and nurses and staff came running. They burst into the ward fearing the worst and were relieved and overjoyed to see their patient had regained consciousness and beginning to recover and soon jelly and juice was placed on the table they'd wheeled into place in front of him.

Although still a little groggy, Brendon could feel his strength and will to live returning and, on the whole, physically, apart from a minor headache, he felt fine but his attitude to life had changed forever. They all chatted for a while and suddenly, having just heard of his recovery, Roxy and Stephanie arrived in uniform and rushed to hug and kiss him. There was laughter, jubilation and relief in the room and Brendon's mind kept slipping back to his out of body state and seeing his friends in a completely new light remembering the parts they had played in that previous incarnation.

The doctor who had operated on Brendon entered the room and shook his hand as he welcomed him back to the land of the living. He told Brendon he'd been extremely worried about Brendon's recovery as they feared they'd lost him a couple of times during the operation. Brendon thanked him for the success of his exceptional surgery and for saving his life which the doctor passed off graciously.

'Lucky you were in such great shape to start with,' the doctor said. 'That bullet was millimetres away from permanent brain damage or death.' And then, reverting back to his standard professionalism, he insisted Brendon be given peace and quiet and the chance to rest. Donald assumed the doctor meant only the others were to leave but he was sternly ordered from the room with the promise he could visit Brendon in a few hours time.

Brendon lay in bed recounting his near-death, out-of-body experience and felt a renewed respect for life in its many facets. He knew he would never talk to Donald about his experience because Donald had his own journey and choices to make this time around and he didn't want his choices to be influenced. He also knew he could never be the same as he was before the coma now that he'd been given the privilege of an insight into another realm of existence that he had always suspected but know knew of as a certainty. He did wish though that he'd been allowed to discover how he had become an artist and if indeed he had in some way played a part in the Renaissance period. Oh well, he thought, I guess I'll have to follow the path I've chosen as Donald will and see where it leads us. But now I know there's a reason for everything and maybe one chapter is closed but who knows where the next chapter will take me.

His eyes became heavy and sleep overcame him.

The next day, Donald discovered him even brighter and stronger and said the doctor had assured him that he was well on the mend and should be able to be discharged very soon. Brendon was pleased and asked Donald how much longer they had left on their tourist visa.

'Only a few more days,' Donald replied.

Stephanie and Roxy offered to drive the Jeep back to Istanbul so that wasn't a worry and he'd change their flight bookings to suit their last day in Turkey.

'That's great,' Brendon replied. 'The car hire company agreed to have the Jeep delivered back to Athens when I booked it but there's just one more thing we have to do before we leave and that will mean a short drive in the country.

Two days later, Brendon was discharged and Donald drove the Jeep to the hospital entrance.

'Where to?' Donald asked. 'To the apartment?'

'No,' Brendon replied, 'you are going to take us to Troy.'

'What, now?' Donald asked in amazement. 'Don't you think you should rest up for a bit before the flight?'

Brendon shook his head. 'No, we've got to go now. This is really important. Listen,' he said before Donald could complain further, 'Alexander the Great and his army walked or rode horses for thousands of miles to conquer this country. Surely we can drive a few miles to pay our respects.'

Donald shrugged and started the motor. 'It's only another fucking ruin,' he said.

'Ah, no,' Brendon smiled as he patted Donald's shoulder, 'it's a farewell to arms.'

Chapter 28

On the highway down to Canakkale, the countryside looked no different to what it had on their first trip even though so much had happened to them in the meantime but Brendon felt an even closer association. They stopped again in the town for their usual coffee and pastry at another cafe they found on the square before driving the next thirty-five miles on to the ruins. 'I don't think we'll have time to stay the night as we planned last time,' Brendon said, as they sipped their coffee.

'Maybe next time we visit Turkey,' Donald replied.

'You expect there'll be a next time?' Brendon asked incredulously. 'I'd have thought you'd seen enough of the place.'

'I don't know,' Donald answered, thoughtfully. 'If not Turkey then somewhere in the Middle East. I really have an affinity to the country and the people and when I saw the desperation and suffering of those refugees streaming across the border; the women and the children and the old people, who just

284

wanted to get on with living their ordinary lives, something rang a bell. The poor bastards are continuously shat on by the powerful and they don't have the strength, education or the ability to stand up for themselves.'

'This is a bit of a change in thinking for you, isn't it?' Brendon said. 'I mean you've been pretty much out for yourself, like most of us.'

Donald nodded, almost ashamedly. 'That's true but it's got to change. I've been talking to Roxy and Steph a lot while we were waiting to see if you were ever going to come back to us and they explained to me why they were so committed in their work. They started me thinking and,' he paused unsure of his intentions, 'I know this sounds a bit naive but it made me think about how the ordinary people of the world are always the ones who suffer the most. Leaders are sometimes elected or powerful factions just take over and force the ordinary people to do as they're told; even in countries that are supposed to be democratic. The scum always seem to rise to the top.'

'That's always been the way,' Brendon said wryly, remembering he and Donald had done exactly that when they were Alexander and Hephaestion. 'The strong will always lead the weak, my friend. Power has always conquered and corrupted. That's the way of mankind. You think you can change that?'

'No,' Donald said, 'I'm not that much of an idiot but we tend to forget there are a lot of ordinary people who choose to do their best to help the ones who are exploited. They bring in medical supplies, food, arrange clean drinking water and make the life of the destitute just a little bit better; like Roxy and Stephanie and the hundreds of other unsung people who just want to help and show a little kindness to those who won't ever have that power.'

'My God, you're turning into another Mother Teresa,' Brendon laughed.

Donald blushed and looked uncomfortable. 'Don't shit on my parade,' he retorted defensively. 'I'd just like to help, that's all.' He paused and then announced his considered decision. 'I want to work for an aid group,' he announced in firm resolve. 'Roxy and Steph are having a word with *Sans Frontières*.'

Brendon looked at him and saw he really was serious. Maybe this was a part of Donald's lesson to learn in this incarnation; selfless compassion. He'd been one of the greatest conquerors the world had ever seen and had forgotten the cost to the people he'd conquered and subjugated. He thought about how Donald had tried to save the young and innocent Ishtar by risking his own life which ended in his brutal rape.

'And what about me – us?' Brendon asked tentatively.

'We'll always be together no matter how many miles apart we are,' Donald replied solemnly and then added, 'But look, you're a great artist, you could work anywhere in the world. Art is very powerful. You could use that talent to highlight the suffering; the wrongs. Bring it to the notice of people who just sit around feeling the problem is too great for them to do anything about. Even if your work could bring some attention to the needs of others, spur them on to actually speak out or do something about it; join the thousands of others who are quietly trying to help the undeveloped world in their small way to show we're all in this together and each of us really does have a responsibility to our fellow man. It would be something. Other people are doing their small bit to help, why not us?'

Brendon thought of the obstacles. 'What about your football career?

'My contract is up and I haven't re-signed yet,' Donald responded.

This sudden epiphany was too much for Brendon to cope with at the moment so he deferred a definite decision. 'Okay, let's talk about it when we get home,' he said. 'This would mean a whole new way of life for us both, you realise, and I don't think we should rush into it.'

'But you will think about it?' Donald asked, hopefully, 'because I've definitely made up my mind.

'I'll think about it,' Brendon assured him; wondering if this too would be part of their next journey. 'Now,' he said, changing the subject, 'we've got to find a florist and be on our way.' He rose from his chair.

'You're going to buy me flowers?' Donald asked incredulously. 'Are they throwing a ball in Troy?'

'God knows what I'm going to get to go with that outfit,' Brendon laughed, referring to the sweaty khaki shorts and shirt Donald was wearing.

The sky was overcast with the promise of a storm as they parked the Jeep in the tourist parking area near the ruins of Troy. Brendon grabbed his backpack as they got out. They were amazed at the magnificent desolation of what was once such an important and powerful city on the plains of Troy. They passed another replica of the Trojan horse, refusing the disconsolate guides who were touting their services, and Donald followed Brendon who obviously had a destination in mind. They passed other tourists who were hurrying towards the car park in an effort to escape the impending storm but both men ignored them, becoming introspective as they walked through the ruins as if transported back into another time. They were heading for the seashore and a line of several high tumuli, large mounds of earth often thought of as ancient burial mounds, and Brendon stopped as if looking for a particular one. He pointed to a particularly high tumulus.

'That one,' he announced, leading them both toward the hill. They climbed the mound and stood looking out to sea. 'This is the spot where Achilles and his lover, Patroclos, were buried,' he announced confidently. 'Below this spot they'll eventually find a golden larnax holding the bones and ashes of Achilles and Patroclos. They were lovers and chose to be buried together through eternity. Alexander the Great visited here with his lover, Hephaestion, and laid wreaths of flowers on the spot and then ran naked around the tomb in tribute. I think we should do the same.'

Donald looked around at a few remaining determined, middle-aged women tourists still inspecting the ruins. 'I don't think you're quite up to running around a fucking hill, mate, and I don't think those women would approve if we stripped off and did the same thing,' he said ruefully.

'Maybe not,' Brendon conceded, as he opened his backpack and withdrew the two white roses he had purchased in Canakkale, 'but we can leave our tribute.'

'Anyway, how do you know this is the right spot?' Donald asked dubiously, looking up at the threatening dark clouds above them.

'Because you and I have been here before,' Brendon replied with a smile.

'You're not onto that reincarnation shit again, are you?' Donald sighed, wearily.

Brendon ignored the remark and handed one of the roses to Donald and dropped to his knees and placed his rose on the highest spot of the tumulus. Donald, heaving another sigh, dropped next to him and repeated the action, placing his rose next to Brendon's, the stems overlapping. Solemnly they looked at each other and Brendon smiled and said, 'Well, here's to the next time.'

There was a sudden roll of thunder followed by a brilliant streak of lightning and above them, the God Zeus smiled down.

The End

Bryon Williams, ex-stage and television actor, script writer, producer, director turned novelist, has now retired to a Retirement Village in Brisbane. Two of his previous novels, *The Grumpy Old Withered of Oz*, a comedic, semi-autobiographical book about the frustrations of ageing and life as his wife's carer in the not-so-fast lane of the Zzzzzzzzz Generation, and *The Twilight Escort Agency*, an hilarious and bawdy account of a mythical escort agency for the 'more mature' client, have enjoyed very positive independent reader response, as has this novel, the whimsical comedy crime-fantasy, ideal for cat lovers, *Code Name: Millicent – The Cat Intelligence Agent Who Came Out of the Cold*.

Tourist from the Light, an intriguing paranormal romance with an underlying theme of a thought-provoking alternative spiritual philosophy, followed. His fifth novel, *The Burning Boy*, is an exciting action/crime page-turner based on the horrors that haunt an ex-Vietnam War cameraman who returns to Australia in the mid seventies and becomes inadvertently involved in a sophisticated and lethal people-smuggling racket.

Bryon's beloved wife of 45 years, Marie, suffered a disastrous stroke in 2000 and he retired to become her full-time carer until she passed on in 2014. Bryon went on to write a memoir of his career and his married life, *A Light at the End*, which received numerous 5-star favourable reviews.

With the legalisation of gay marriage and acceptance of sexual equality, Bryon then changed course and wrote *Naked Warriors*, a gay, erotic love story based on Bryon's belief in Reincarnation.

Intrigued and inspired by an old friend's unresolved story of the tragic murder of her daughter in 1988, they collaborated to co-write *Not in the Public Interest*, published in 2019.